ADVANCE PRAISE

# The HISTORY of RAIN

"This is what it means to care. A story of trauma and order, chaos and beauty, reality and fantasy, *The History of Rain* constructs a path from the trenches of WWI to the film sets and opulent estates of Golden Age Hollywood. Along the way, the story grapples with massive forces: nature and time, love and longing, public and private space. Malone is like his character, a master of cultivation, and this book, like the gardens it imagines, is a wonder of patience and intricate attention. Wander through and try to take it all in. Everywhere you look, there is more than you expect."

**–Alexander MacLeod**, Giller Prize–shortlisted author of *Light Lifting*

"Transporting and profound, *The History of Rain* is a haunting tale of love, hope, truth, and beauty lost and found in unexpected places. This captivating novel had me turning pages late into the night."

**–Ami McKay,** bestselling author of *The Birth House*

"Reader, let this beautifully crafted story transport you on a quest for love and belonging through war-ravaged Europe, the razzle dazzle of Old Hollywood, and the enchantment of grand landscape gardens. Evocative of both D. H. Lawrence and F. Scott Fitzgerald, Stephens Gerard Malone has created a sumptuous story of unrelenting tension, passion, and heartbreak."

**–Christy Ann Conlin,** author of *The Speed of Mercy* and *Watermark*

"*The History of Rain* is a spellbinding tale of enchantment, deception, and the impulses and illusions that make us human. Stephens Gerard Malone is a master, his writing a marvel of breathtaking tautness and force as he charts the darkness of war-ravaged Europe and the gilt, sun-drenched surfaces of Old Hollywood. A novel as dazzling as the gardens at the heart of it—astonishing."

–**Carol Bruneau**, award-winning author of *Brighten the Corner Where You Are*


"A moving and compassionate tale of war's devastation, the moral cost of survival, and one man's search for love. Writing with cinematic clarity, Stephens Gerard Malone proves again that he is a master of narrative tension and a first-rate historical novelist. This is a novel that leaves an indelible mark on the reader."

–**Ian Colford**, award-winning author of *A Dark House & Other Stories*

# The
# History
# *of*
# Rain

Vagrant Press is an imprint of
Nimbus Publishing Limited
3660 Strawberry Hill Street, Halifax, NS, B3K 5A9
(902) 455-4286 nimbus.ca

Printed and bound in Canada
NB1542

*This story is a work of fiction. Names, characters, incidents, and places, including organizations and institutions, are used fictitiously.*

Editor: Kate Juniper
Editor for the press: Whitney Moran
Cover design: Jenn Embree & Whitney Moran
Interior design: Rudi Tusek & Jenn Embree

Library and Archives Canada Cataloguing in Publication

Title: The history of Rain / Stephens Gerard Malone.
  Names: Malone, Stephens Gerard, 1957- author.
  Identifiers: Canadiana (print) 20210214988 | Canadiana (ebook) 20210215011 |
  ISBN 9781771089791 (softcover) | ISBN 9781771089807 (EPUB)
  Subjects: LCGFT: Novels.
  Classification: LCC PS8626.A455 H57 2021 | DDC C813/.6—dc23

Nimbus Publishing acknowledges the financial support for its publishing activities from the Government of Canada, the Canada Council for the Arts, and from the Province of Nova Scotia. We are pleased to work in partnership with the Province of Nova Scotia to develop and promote our creative industries for the benefit of all Nova Scotians.

# The
# History
# *of*
# Rain

## STEPHENS
## GERARD MALONE

Vagrant
PRESS

*Taraxacum*

# 1915

The corporal, the one wearing the Red Cross and pulling the limbs of dead horses off the young soldier, fired over the children's heads.

*Thieving beggars.* Tearing buttons off frozen-stiff coats and pulling gold bands from hands no longer attached. They twirled and made faces at each other in the snow, little more than bones and want. At the echoing shots, the children, like crows, flew only so far before perching on tree stumps with cold stares to wait.

"You think he's a kraut?" the driver asked, eyeing the bloody young soldier covered in horsemeat, then opening the rear doors to the lorry.

"Not this far west of the front." The corporal gagged as he removed the last of the horseflesh from the body beneath it. "Jesus. He's just a lad."

"They'd stuff toddlers into cannons if they was willing to sign up," said the driver, unrolling the stretcher. Standing beside the corporal, he spit a long wet stream black with tobacco. "Fuck me King and country, where's his bloody face?"

The two men looked at each other.

"Got anything to cover him with?"

"Only expected dead ones, mate."

The corporal took off his coat though the snow was thickening and wet.

"This one'll wish he was."

Blood would ruin it, but no man, no matter what he'd done, deserved to be carried off the field with his arse out.

The soldier groaned and blinked at the rapidly parting grey above.

"You're a lucky bastard, son. Germans found ya, they'd shoot."

But from the looks on the two faces staring down at him, he wasn't lucky at all.

They slid the soldier, naked under the corporal's coat, into the back of the ambulance.

"General Pétain's men've been out this way. You think he's a Frenchy? *Que faisons-nous vous appeler?"* the driver shouted at the soldier.

Nothing.

"C'mon there, soldier," said the corporal, gently folding over the flap of the man's face and wrapping it with gauze. "Doc'll put you back together in no time. You'll want to get back to your regiment. Don't want to miss all the fun, eh?"

"Give us your name," said the driver over the sputtering engine.

*You hear the cries a horse makes, drowning in its own blood? Lungs burning with sulfur? I'm dead to you. No name to give....*

The corporal delivered the body a numbing jab of morphine, the ambulance rocking as it pitched over uneven ground.

What remained of the rough and pitted road was unforgiving. The soldier, bouncing against the stretcher in the back, pressed his hand against the icy glass under the roll of canvas and watched, as somewhere between the blue inky clouds and the city of Caen, the snow became rain.

WHEN THE BACK DOORS TO the ambulance wrenched open, Rain raised an arm to shield himself from the blustering showers outside. Heavy grey walls under low dull skies. Automobiles, wagons, and lorries choked the courtyard. A sodden flag clung to the corner. *Enlist, young man! King and country! See the world!* Horseshit steamed on cobbles. The driver jumped out and bounded up stairs under a columned portico. The corporal saluted a captain hurrying by, who flinched at the sight of the bandaged soldier, then wiped his face. Over here, someone yelled.

"You can rest easy now, mate," the corporal said, blowing into and then rubbing his hands.

But morphine wears off.

▲▲▲

DARKNESS.

Pain.

The horses—

*Kill me kill me kill me.*

A-face-not-even-a-mother-could-love.

I'd-rather-wish-for-death.

Muffled duty disguised as pity, clock-like footsteps down a cold stone hall, coming and going, loud and fading. Flame and fire and mortar flash diffused through gauze bandages, but-rest-easy-son-it's-only-morning, come to burn him alive with agony so devouring, the memory alone was agony. *But rip the skin off inch-by-inch I'll not bow to King stand for country kneel to God, I'll not scream, I won't remember I'll never tell never never never—* surviving, the only war being fought here, soldier—until the jabbing surrender and bliss of abyss from numbing poppies *and if I pass Him on the fall down, I'm asking what was the big deal in Gethsemane. Suffering? You can't know a boy's suffering—surely this makes me a man now—because you're God, and eating Your own body and blood is nothing compared to drinking from oozing stitches and draining sutures, so fuck you,* but a strong grip there for the Son of God.

"Easy buddy, just the ether talking, it'll be over soon," said the orderly as Rain inhaled sweetness and let go. "Ladies love a man with a scar, and this surgeon's the best at stitching lads like you back together. Have you back in the field in no time."

"Don't you believe that," said the man with hollow cheeks and a rather vain moustache sharing the room with Rain. "Butchers. You know what this place was? A sanitarium for the French Disease. A Hail Mary full of grace just before they cut your cock off."

He spit on the floor.

"Nuns all pious and holy saying that's what you get for eating forbidden fruit, as if those slags opened their mouth for anything but a prayer—"

"There, there," said the woman standing over him, scissors in hand.

"Ah, ignore her. She thinks I'm crazy, all the Frenchys do. But I'll tell you this...French army? Almost blew this place up storing munitions out back. And that doctor? Bloody Yank. Worse—a ginger. Might do seeing that shade on a dolly bird mincing about Trafalgar Square, but no self-respecting man has a top that colour."

Both of the man's legs were gone from above the knees and the stumps, newly sutured and bandaged, seeped with brownish red. As soon as the Sister's footsteps went quiet in the hallway, he pulled his wool puttees out from under his pillow.

"Won't be needing these," he said, braiding the leg wraps together. "Name's Disraeli, mate. Benjamin Disraeli. Pleased to bunk in here with you and I don't give a fuck if you were trying to desert. Pleased for the company, young fellow." He stunk of piss, was too busy with his leg wraps to shake hands.

Rain, criss-crossed with stitches and swollen, sat by the window watching the wet snow turn the courtyard to mud. She caught his eye as, born from the shadows, her silky golden curls under dirty kerchief shone in the dim light, and when the girl's shoe came off in the muck, she laughed. Head right back, standing on one foot, and she laughed. Sodden and grey and yet, joy. Then she was gone, her footprints slowly filling with water until Rain wondered if she was real and had ever walked barefoot along a beach.

Disraeli, holding up his braided puttees, asked if Rain had a way out. "Every soldier's duty to escape, lad."

"But we're not prisoners."

"Between you and me, I told them I'm Belgian."

Disraeli's fingers braided quickly, unravelled it all and braided again as the late spring fell hard and wet against the panes of the two tall windows in the room.

"Won't do if the Huns get me, bad for the war effort. I've got to get back to London. Very important, me."

"Oh? Who are you?"

He stopped braiding, his tightly-clenched fists shaking, and almost spit when he said, "Boy, I'm the fucking Prime Minister."

IN THE MORNING AS RAIN sat by the window Sister Wicks wheeled in the usual tray. The other boys in his regiment, corn-fed with prairie smiles or factory lads daringly eschewing undershirts, all now in bits and pieces, would have howled and winked over the Sister's long face, her big teeth. She was worth another joke or two for wearing that hat pinned with suffragette colours.

Disraeli grimaced as she examined his bloody stumps and berated him for the careless use of his bedpan.

"I'll thank you, Sister, to show me the proper respect due His Majesty's minister."

"Perhaps you'll try the wheelchair today, your Lordship?"

Disraeli looked ahead, his jaw set.

When she unwrapped the bandages around Rain's head, he looked for a widening of her eyes in horror, but the woman had seen too much beauty stitched back in mangled pieces and betrayed nothing.

"Doctor Elliott says you can start taking your meals in the dining hall," she said after trimming the edges off the newly wound gauze. "Do you good. Says you can't hide up here forever." She dropped the scissors with a clang into an enamelled bowl. "Americans for you. Full of crazy ideas."

"He'd rather just stare at the courtyard," said Disraeli.

Not the courtyard. Her. She was back again. Blonde curls, one-sided smile. No one else smiled in a place like this, not like that. Not peaches-and-cream, not even worth the fall of Troy. But dance floors would part for her smile. Not that he could dance, or that she'd even sign his name to her card if he could. But a dream wants what a dream wants and in this world, a dream was an act of defiance. She must've been cold with only the wrap about her.

Sister Wicks pushed Rain's chair away from the sill and unlatched the window. "You there, yes! I see you. You've been warned off these grounds. Now be away with you."

The girl tugged on her shawl and then ran.

"Ah, leave her, Sister," said Disraeli. "Girl's got a right to earn her bread."

"Like maggots to carrion," she said to no one in particular. "All these poor wounded officers here not thinking right, and her trying to get herself to England."

"Close the fucking window."

After Sister Wicks was gone, Disraeli poured tea from the pot she'd left.

"Go on," he offered Rain. No cup, but he could drink from the saucer.

"Don't let Sister's English charm fool you. That bitch is an Austrian spy. I'd shove my pistol in her mouth and pull the trigger, but they got my gun, bloody Bolsheviks. Know where I could get my hands on one?"

Rain didn't think so, but he wondered if he should tell Sister about the rope made from soldiers' leggings hidden under Disraeli's mattress.

RAIN STUMBLED INTO THE GARDEN the day he found the feather in his porridge. Not the white of a coward, but close enough. Could be from one of the pigeons getting in past the crudely repaired hole in the ceiling, chasing the sisters hither and yon, and he might have believed that, except for the other wounded who crowded every table but his, staring at him and thanking a god no one really believed in anymore for only losing a limb or two, and not honour. And a face. Not that Rain figured he'd really lost much in that regard. Except maybe the ability to disappear.

He escaped the whispers in the columned cloisters behind the south wing of Bon Sauveur Hospital, where neither patients nor army nor the sisters seemed to wander. Curved and sweeping, with splintered granite walls and rafters sheathed in slate shattered and charred at each end by some mistaken blast, it housed sparrows and grackles, and the broken-tiled fields were littered with sandstone pedestals and the corpses of copses, rusting wagons, and carriages. A few hungry horses flicked at flies with their tails. Here he was alone, except for the annoying presence of that old man.

Wide-brimmed straw hat, trousers secured with a doubled length of twine. Dried mud clinging to his shirt, unless it poured, and then the shirt clung to a frame that once knew a bigger man. Now so frail one of these hardy gusts that still smelled of Dover might take him down. His face was uneven, deeply lined, and he took painfully slow steps across the muddy ruts near the picked-clean carcass of a horse. His spade stuck into the ground as he held the wooden handle hand over hand, and then he lowered himself to his knees to scoop a handful of muck and from his pocket, drop a seed. A few more planted here and there, the old man took hold of the spade and pulled himself up.

"CAN'T SAY I'VE SEEN HIM," said Doctor Elliott, cupping his hands around a match as he touched it to the end of a cigarette. "Lots of people come and go around here."

He'd scheduled the next of Rain's surgeries—still experimental—for the day after next. The details as he described them left Rain wondering if his dead comrades had not fared better: a piece of his rib cartilage would be stitched under the skin in his forehead; and when that was sufficiently grafted, it would be turned to form a bridge for the nose, the last piece of his face to be reconstructed. The cheeks and lips, the doctor said, had healed as well as could be expected.

The pain?

On bad days, the screaming in his head drowned out all thoughts of death. On good days, he listened.

Since the warmer weather the doctor met Rain in the courtyard where he stretched his arms across the back of the bench, eyes closed against the sun. No collar, shirt top open. No wonder that when Sister Wicks accompanied the red-haired doctor on his rounds, hands knotted together, her chin jutted out in British disapproval.

"How's the ringing?" he asked.

In his ears? Gone now, although Rain swore that everything still smelled like dead men's shit and the food tasted like sulfur.

"That's the mind playing tricks on you. To be expected after what you've experienced. Any memories?"

Lots, but he wasn't telling. Only that morning, the first bits of spring-yellow in the mud pit outside the window, and the church bells in the town recalled Sunday school and yellow flowers trembling in his hands, picked by the charred remains of a quarryman's hut. Like holding the sun. And a grey woman with a grey face and a grey heart saying he'd sinned, and for what? *Taraxacum officinale.* Missing the Lord's Communion, for weeds! Better throw them on the ground and the girls dancing in rings stepped on them. Husha. Husha. Then the nun dragged him to a washbasin and scrubbed his hands for penance until his nails bled. Oh My God I Am Heartily Sorry For Having Offended Thee. On the chalkboard, she drew a circle with a hole in the middle. *Children, this is the boy's soul.* Pointing to the hole, *and here is his sin.* Venial sins you can colour in with a piece of chalk. Mortal sins? Mea culpa mea culpa may God help yeah. Did God have a soul, and how big was His hole? All this Rain could have told the doctor, but then he'd know he could remember.

"No matter. Who wouldn't want to forget the war? Clean slate, eh private? But the mind doesn't work that way. We both know that's not fair to those waiting for some word about you. I bet your family is worried, huh? Maybe even a sweetheart?"

*No.*

"And there's those men, your fellow soldiers. You could help put their kin at ease, tellin' how their boys were at the end."

How were they? They died laughing. That's what Rain'd say
if he had to. Bastards barely even knew what hit them. Standing in
ankle-deep piss and mud, wearing shit-faced grins of privilege and
beauty. The looks on their faces when they realized it was over—

The doctor tapped Rain on the arm. "But all in good time,
right? I say we stop worrying about when your memory's going
to come back. It will, one day, you'll see, then we'll get you where
you belong."

Rain hoped not.

The red-haired man sat up and tapped his thighs, signalling
the end of the session, but Rain stayed put.

"Something else on your mind, soldier?"

"Why does he do it?"

"Who?" Doctor Elliot glanced at a watch he pulled from his
waistcoat.

"That old man I told you about, digging. Every day."

"Does it bother you?"

"No. But look around. Just seems...pointless."

"The sisters tell me that before the war, people came 'round
on Sundays and picnicked in the gardens." He gazed across the
mud and broken turf and wounded trees, as if it were all normal.
"You wouldn't know that now from looking at the place. Maybe
he's one of the caretakers. Men like that, it's a duty for them. If
he interests you so—"

"He doesn't. "

"You know, wouldn't hurt to give the old fellow a hand.
Good for a man to get his hands in the ground. Grew up on a
farm myself. Wisconsin." The doctor smiled as if the memory of
home was a happy one. Lucky him. "Get your mind off things.
Can't have you sitting around all day."

Rain was about to object.

"In fact, that's an order, soldier."

🝑🝑🝑

THE OLD GARDENER WAS JUST as mad as the legless man in the next bed. On his knees in mud every day, and for what? No one remembered what this place was like before the war. Look at it. No one cared. Warhorses and wagons of wounded had beaten whatever garden was here under their hooves and wheels ringed with iron. Yet here was this old fool, burnt brown from the sun or trembling in the icy fog, day after day.

"Why do you do this?"

The old man said nothing. Maybe he didn't understand English. Maybe he was deaf. Finally, he glanced over his shoulder. "So, you with no face finally speaks."

Rain tossed his cigarette into a muddy puddle and climbed down the crumbling stairs. "The weeds grow faster than you can dig."

The gardener looked about him. "Yup."

"Waste of time."

"Give the earth your rage, young man, she'll give you flowers."

"That doesn't make any sense."

The old fellow didn't care to argue.

"Hey, where are you going?"

He followed the old man to the shed behind the chapel, the one with a hole in the roof, heard him muttering about rusting hoes and rakes and shovels, and a wheelbarrow with a cracked wooden wheel.

"Some mending, oil, and sharpening, and they'd be good to use," the old man said presumptuously, "but if you're going to do anything about it, you'd better mind the pigeons, they're roosting overhead."

### ♦♦♦

THE OLD MAN WAITED FOR Rain where the cloisters finished in a set of low steps. Nearby, bits of papery skin still clinging to the ribs of the horse's skeleton fluttered in the breeze. By his feet, three clay pots sprouted budding twigs.

"Oak," he said. "From seeds. I hid them in the cellar when I thought the Germans were coming, but then they never did. Let's plant them out there, by the wall, so the roots will stay moist and they'll have shelter from the wind. Someday, they'll give shade. A garden needs sun, but it also needs shade."

"If they survive...take years for that to happen."

"If it's haste you want, become a baker."

Rain squinted doubtfully at the distant spot. "Why not plant them here? The building can protect them from the wind."

"Plant wisely, young man. Young fools like you are liable to step on them before they get that big."

They carried the saplings over to the rotting horse. Rain bristled and muttered at having to push the unwieldy wheelbarrow across the muddy field.

"These oaks, my boy, will outlive foolish empires. Trust me."

The gardener showed Rain where to dig, then, with great difficulty, lowered himself to his knees and gently tapped the saplings into the ground. Not in a line, but clustered, with one just offside.

"Men want order," he said. "Not God. Best make it look like He had a hand in this."


DISRAELI'S DINNER SAT UNTOUCHED BY his bed when Rain returned.

"It's that donkey. Puts me off my food, she does." He meant Sister Wicks. "Here, you eat it. I know you hate going down to the hall, blokes staring at ya."

After Rain ate the cold potatoes and the soup stringy with leek while Disraeli finished with his smoking, he poured tea for them from the steaming pot.

"Put your head out the door and see if that bitch is out there, would ya? No? Good. I need you to help me with something. In the closet, my uniform. Can you get it out for me? Help me dress. It's time for me to shut that woman up and take this new chair out for a spin."

"You up to it?"

Disraeli stubbed out his cigarette in the soup bowl. "Let's not be a pansy about a roll down the hall."

Rain laid the man's tunic and trousers across the end of the bed.

"Doctor Elliott says working in the garden is good for me. Maybe I could wheel you out there too. You could watch, get some sun. The old gardener out there speaks nonsense, well, mostly nonsense. A lot about God. Still, better than sitting in here staring at these walls."

"You talk too much, lad. Parliament will be sitting any day now. War needs ending. Be a good fellow and get my shaving kit from the dresser. Top drawer. There's a mirror inside." Disraeli rubbed his chin. "You'll have to find me some hot water and soap."

When Rain returned with a steaming bowl, Disraeli had already put on his shirt, so he held the mirror while the older man shaved. Then he helped him into his tunic.

"What about your trousers?"

"Get them on me and let them hang. At least it'll look like I'm all here. My collar straight, soldier?"

Seemed to be.

"Good. Now help me into this contraption."

Rain let the man put his arm about his shoulder, then he carefully reached under Disraeli's two stumps.

The man flinched, but nodded impatiently. "It's nothing, mate. Let's do this."

Rain sat the man in the chair.

Disraeli took hold of the wheels and cautiously pushed himself around the room.

"Not a bad ride is this. Almost marvellous. Now, young man, stick your head out the door and make sure that horse-faced twat isn't leading the charge up and down the halls."

Rain gave the all-clear.

"Good. Then let me out."

The soldier wheeled himself into the hall and towards the inner balustrade from where he could look down into the entrance hall.

"Good heavens, man, I forgot my hat. Run back to the room and get it for me."

Rain smiled at the Prime Minister's change of spirits as he reached for the top shelf. His stitches made him pay for that. Or maybe it was thinking about getting back to Methuselah out in the fields. Tomorrow he wanted Rain to help him shore up some masonry so they could dig a perennial bed, and then—

After the *snap*, a bang, like a large sack of potatoes hitting a wall. Disraeli's empty wheelchair slowly rolled back through the door.

When Rain reached the balustrade he clutched at the braided puttees, hidden under Disraeli's shirt and hastily secured about the stone railing, and tried to stop the man from swinging as he hung by his neck over the heads of the terrified sisters.

RAIN WATCHED THE SHROUDED BODY in the back of the horse-drawn wagon being pulled past the iron gates.

"Was he a friend of yours?" asked the old man, knotting the scarf about his neck.

"I knew nothing about him."

"And yet you weep. Come. Let's not waste those tears."

The work, Rain was grateful for. Anything to get him out of his room, away from the empty bed next to his. If he rose early enough, he could be down in the dining hall before even the sisters made their rounds, thus avoiding the looks and comments from the other men. Sooner or later he'd be called out. Some officer hell-bent on reconciling the missing and the dead. Rain dreaded that. Not standing up to the others had got his face blown off, but surely saved his life. If you considered looking like a sack of pulped turnips much of a life. He'd not endure returning to a full hall for dinner each night, so the porridge, slices of bread thickly buttered, milk, and as much heavily sugared tea as he could manage would be his only meal of the day, eaten at the table in the farthest corner where the window overlooked the fields he worked with the old man, and he could watch the girl with the golden hair.

When he saw her staring through the dining room window, not at the two orderlies, but at their plates heaped with steaming eggs and boiled potatoes, he realized she was older than he had first thought. An English rose, fifteen, maybe sixteen, he had heard one of the men say of her with the self-satisfied look of having partaken, but a bob well spent. Drops her knickers faster than you can say if-you-please. A few shillings, mate, and if you say you'll get her across the Channel, she'll give you the full night.

Rain pushed away his plate. Poor kid. Shivering in a tattered shawl that could do nothing against the morning cold, just trying to get home. Like Disraeli. Maybe she'd get tired of surviving too. He hoped not. Carefully he concealed a loaf of bread in his tunic on his way out, and took a bottle of milk.

She started to run when she saw him step through the casement window, but Rain followed, and soon found her, crouched behind the shrubs that clung to the pavilion's hard granite edges.

He handed her the bread and milk.

"For me?"

He nodded.

The girl looked unsure, but hungry. She began to undo the buttons on her dress.

"No, what are you doing?"

"For the food—"

"No, no."

The girl looked confused.

"Take it. Go. Sisters mustn't find you here."

SHE DIDN'T SHOW PITY FOR him, nor did she turn away from looking when she brought Rain the coat.

"Lily," she said, when he asked her name.

*Lill-lee.* Lilting, like the first songs of spring birds full-throated in days of plenty, ripe berries and easy worms and warm nights, not a thought that winter might return. Lily. A lily bloom only gave you one day of delight, the old gardener had warned disapprovingly. *Lill-lee.* She said she'd been named by her papa, a military hero long dead now, after his favourite flower.

The coat was oilskin, with a hood.

"You'll be dry," she said.

"But why?"

"You're not like the sisters. And the other men, they only want—what men want—"

Rain ran his fingers over the canvas-like fabric.

"Oh, don't worry. He didn't die of anything catchy."

Rain put on the coat and Lily made him turn around to show her how it fit.

The coat had a hole, just above the chest, wiped clean. "Sister was going to put it in the poor box, but it's—well, if you don't mind me noticing, it's very large, so I knew it would fit you."

"You took it?"

"No one saw."

Lily sat on the step, back from where the water poured off the roof, and folded her dirty skirt between her legs. "Is it true what they say about you? That they found you buried under a pile of horses, and everyone else in your regiment dead?"

What about being found out of uniform? Did she know about that? A coward? Wanting to desert? That's what they were all really whispering. He'd have defended himself, sullied the memory of all those pretty boys in his regiment, if not for the shame. If not for the truth. How they had stripped him, the poor country boy, and greased him for a *pig catch*, they called it, made him run for their sport through the trenches so his bored chums could have a laugh. Even took bets. Haw-haw. The horses whinnying just before that shell exploded.

The sweetness of her voice pulled him back. "I'm sorry. I shouldn't have asked."

Spring may have come, but some days, like today, what fell from the sky clung to winter.

"Nice of you to bring me the coat."

Rain shoved the spade back into the earth and tried not to look at her. Better she go now. Let any words between them be the ones Rain pretended to say to her, which she'd surely laugh at if she heard them. Still, he liked to think them. Kind nothings he could make over into something to remember after his bandages came off and revulsion drove her away. Serve you right, he imagined Disraeli saying, girls like her always smile with a hand out before they lift their skirts.

"What's that you're doing?" she asked.

"Making a path."

With the sand and gravel and flagstones he found behind the gardening shed, enough for her walk without muddy shoes.

The old man said there used to be walks all over the grounds, before the military wagons and the ambulances.

"Looks like very hard work. Then what? After you finish with the stone?"

Rain straightened up, feeling the ache of digging, and Sister Wicks's disapproving stare on his back. Wouldn't do the girl well to be caught here with him.

"He wants to restore the gardens, the old man, but...take years for these beds to fill in again. Wagons and horses ruined most everything."

"Is that what you were before the war? A gardener?"

Rain shoved the spade back into the ground, wiped is forehead. "Just helping that old man—he's around here somewhere."

Talking with Lily, it was the most he'd said, Rain figured, since he'd been shipped to France. Stitches still hurt, but it was a good hurt.

She smiled with her reply. "When I was very little, the house across the street from ours belonged to a gardener. He was very kind and sometimes let me and my mother through the gate. I never knew the names of anything Mr. McCauley put in the ground, but he always had colour. Lots of colour. I like that, don't you? And how gardens change. Like a new frock for every season. One should never get bored in a garden. Mr. McCauley often gave my mother cuttings and bulbs, but she wasn't good at growing anything."

Rain liked that smiles came naturally to Lily, and that two of her front teeth turned inward, just a bit. She thrust her hand into the water dripping off the roof.

"Could use those cuttings and bulbs now," he said, his mouth dry. "We prepare beds, but there is nothing to plant."

💧💧💧

SOON BASKETS OF BULBS, TUBERS, cuttings, and even fruit trees with roots wrapped in burlap appeared at the gates, pulled from iron-railed plots hidden down narrow lanes and overflowing clay pots on balconies. Rain was sure Lily never asked for permission, but word was getting about and the offerings kept coming.

No way of knowing from the old man's gnarled face if he was pleased or not by the gifts, but Rain decided he must be, in his own way, as the gardener sketched out an elaborate plan on the dirt floor of the shed while Rain watched from atop a ladder, setting slate tiles in the roof.

"Get some sleep. We begin at dawn," the old man said.

Rain reached for another tile. "My bandages come off tomorrow."

"Takes all day?"

"No. I just thought—"

"What? That I'd not stomach the sight of you? What do I care what you look like. And the garden only cares that you water and weed."

"NOSE TISSUE IS STILL SWOLLEN and there's some infection. But the swelling in your lips has gone down." Doctor Elliott did not conceal his disappointment, though he tried.

Alone in his room with Disraeli's palm-sized shaving mirror, Rain gingerly touched the lines where stitches had grafted back his face, and stared at the onion-sized lump of flesh that was his nose.

Give it time, you'll grow into your new face, the doctor had said.

All this to say he'd done the best he could.

Rain threw the mirror against the wall.

THE SUN MOVED ACROSS THE floor and chased off shadows. Footsteps quickened outside in the hallway. Sister Wicks had come about dinner.

"You must eat, keep up your strength," she said dutifully, looking at the empty bed beside Rain's. It was her way of making sure he wouldn't forget. How could he help dress a man with no legs in a uniform, put him into his wheelchair, and let him wheel away like that? Did he not think he'd hang himself? What had he been thinking?

"Get out." The sound of his own voice startled him.

Glancing at the empty bed, he now grasped the depth of Disraeli's loss. His loss, too. All for what? Kings and emperors, no threat to their faces and legs, carving up countries on a map. He regretted not doing more for the make-believe prime minister, and now regretted that he was not dead too.

Rain had never even learned the man's real name.

"I DON'T CARE WHAT YOU look like," said the old man dismissively the next day. "Just need two strong arms. Much to do."

*And years it'll take to do it*, thought Rain, but it was as good a reason as any to escape the halls reeking of urine and iodine where the wounded clustered to smoke and stare blankly and figure out how to piece together broken dreams. A purpose for hands that could just as easily braid rope out of puttees.

AS RAIN PUSHED THE CUTTING-LOADED wheelbarrow to the south-wing garden where lengths of string marked out an intricate design for the beds, he was sure the field looked larger, the task even more impossible.

"Now mind what you do there as you turn the ground. That's right. That sheep manure keeps the soil rich. It's not what you sow, young man, it's how you sow it."

"But it's mud."

"Yes, the mud you came from and the mud you'll go back to. Treat the cover of your grave with respect."

When Rain's back muscles were knotted from digging, and his hands burned with blisters, the old man took pity and gave him pause while he pointed out the runaway grapes.

"There's rot in the trellis," he said, shaking the wooden beam. "And those vines must be cut back. They'll get into the trees and cover the rooftops. That brings the birds and their shit, and they won't stop at the grapes."

Lunch came, shared from a flour sack tied about the old man's waist. A bottle of red wine, half a loaf of coarse brown bread, ripe cheddar wrapped in newsprint. Although the words of the paper were French, Rain guessed from all the exclamation points that the war machine churned on its merry way.

After they had eaten, the gardener allowed himself a few minutes to lean against the stone wall backing the arbour, where the budding vines dappled the sun that shone on his brown and creased face. From his pocket, he pulled a well-thumbed note-book full of yellowing pages intricately covered with drawings of flowers and follies.

"I keep all my lovelies in here, ideas to help me plan for each spring. Come, learn."

The old fellow's strength and mastery continued to astound Rain as he watched him sketch pieces of stone, faces of statues, a broken shell. *Study the surface. See below the surface. Measure everything with your mind and with a ruler. Learn to see lines and volumes, feel temperature and coarse textures, question form.* But the man gave up nothing about where he'd come from, who he was.

Rain asked once about his life away from Bon Sauveur, but tittle-tattle's for women, the old man replied, and none of the hospital staff had time to know. Yet even with the gardener's brusque and unsentimental words, Rain found himself drawn to him. He had never known his own father, only a mother who said he'd do right by God to lie and enlist even if he was too young, because she wasn't having any more of his mouth to feed. This knotted old gardener was nothing like the fantasy of a father Rain had crafted, no polished wellingtons, no Sunday afternoon fishing trips, no manly beard silvering with age, but his steady ways, his rough but gentle guidance, and more than anything, his appreciation of company, was a comfort Rain had never known.

As SEEDLINGS AND SAPLINGS AND cuttings took hold, the old man fussed like the patriarch of some large unwieldy family, doling out sun and water, turning over leaves and bending back shrubs.

"All your best attention can still amount to naught," he said. "Keep leaves dry, so they don't rot. Sprinkle with garlic water to keep away the pests. And be firm with the hardy. It's not only the weeds you must be vigilant against. Even the most desirable of roses can smother you with their fragrance."

But sometimes, no amount of devotion could beat back the ravages of caterpillars or an unwanted spore, or the cracking of aging limbs. In the orchard, faltering to catch his breath and wipe the sweat beading from under his straw hat, he showed Rain trees where bubbling scabs festered and blistered the bark.

"Take it down," he said, handing Rain the axe, his shaking hands not up to the task.

"Can't you do something? This tree looks like it's been here for ages."

"And let this fungus spread to the whole orchard? Everything has its time. Take it down."

Rain burned the diseased limbs in a pit dug at the far end of the garden, where he tossed in the bones of the horse. The fire burned late, and in the morning he sprinkled the ash around the roses.

The last time he saw the old gardener he gave Rain a warning about the English ivy climbing the south wall of the sanitarium.

"Rip it out,' he had said, walking slowly from the shed as if the weight of the shovel in his hand might tip him over. "You think it looks nice, but ivy blankets the ground until everything dies from no sun. Even the largest oak can be felled by its weight. And never, never let it take hold by the foundations. It'll root into the mortar, weakening it as it climbs."

DOCTOR ELLIOTT'S FRENCH WAS REMARKABLY good, if jarring to hear with that American accent of his. He thanked the Mother Superior and in return received a thin smile that expressed great weariness with anything to do with the war and the continued presence of military men at Bon Sauveur.

"She doesn't know where this gardener of yours is. Claims men used to work the fields as penance, but now they've got the war."

The doctor and Rain walked into the hallway. Rain put his wide-brimmed hat back on, and pulled it down in front. Do what you can to avoid seeing that flicker of revulsion in a passing face.

"How long has it been?" asked Doctor Elliott.

"A few days. Not like him. He's out every morning before dawn."

"And you really know nothing about the man? Family? Where he lives?"

"Nothing."

Gone. Without a word.

"Then I'm sorry. If he was as old as you say, perhaps you should expect the end. Can you continue without him? You've made remarkable progress." He looked out over the extensive grounds. Rain and the gardener had barely weeded through five years of decay. "Surely the old fellow didn't expect to complete the work with just the two of you. Should I rally more men? Could you use the help?"

"No, sir. The other ranks...couldn't I carry on alone?"

At the main doors, Doctor Elliott stopped for a cigarette and eyed Rain doubtfully.

"You're handling your disfigurement well. Working the earth has done wonders for you. With so much to do, you could help other patients who are well enough and willing to work. Think of it as a tribute to your friend, whoever he was." The doctor raised his hand against objections. "That's an order, soldier."

RAIN WISHED THE MAJOR WOULD find some other place to sit and smoke. Older fellow, just arrived at Bon Sauveur, greying blond and the kind of square face the moving pictures would have loved had it not the look of having been recently sandblasted. Rain and the officer never spoke, but just the way Major Lutyen looked at him, stared at him, made Rain feel uneasy. Did he know something about his regiment? How could he? There'd been no survivors but him. Rain was sure, so sure. He wasn't going back, one way or another.

The sisters often talked as if the patients were all deaf, Sister Wicks being the worst, and so it was from her that Rain learned that Major Lutyen was wounded at Lys and came from money—not old money, but merchant's money, mind you. She spoke as if that left the officer dirty, but the other sisters laughed. Times'll be changing, dearie, they said. Money's money, and the more the better. Even finer if it came in the pockets of a distinguished war hero whose injury didn't affect him bringing pleasure to his lady.

Hero maybe, but to Rain it looked like the rich didn't heal any better than the poor. Lutyen was left like all the rest to work on his scowl, crutches at his side, fingers yellowing with nicotine, and thus he watched Rain.

"How much they pay you?" he called out one day.

Rain did not look up from where he knelt, sweat dripping from under his hat into his eyes, arms covered with itchy welts from ant bites.

"No pay."

Lutyen flicked the butt of his cigarette into the grass by Rain, then struggled and cursed at his crutches and hobbled back inside.

Surely the officer had somehow recognized Rain from his regiment, heard the stories of what happened, went to notify Doctor Elliott. Rain's fears raced with his blood—to the sentence of a court martial and, worse, the name he'd relinquished.

He dug late that night, preparing the earth for a row for boxwoods, a hole that looked like a grave. But no armed guard came. No one came.

The major did not take his familiar spot on the porch for several days after that. Maybe he'd been discharged and returned to England. Rain was hopeful, but no. Lutyen came back to his bench as Rain used a sharpened piece of wood to score the stems of several shrubs he'd just transplanted.

"Why do you do that?"

Rain did not meet the eye of the officer. "Wounding the stalks helps the roots grow, makes the plant stronger."

He had learned how to do this, like all related things, from the gardener. Though it would be a lot easier if the doctor let him use a knife.

"I SEEN YOU NATTERING TO Major Lutyen," Sister Wicks told Rain when she came to change the bed linens. "I hope you're not bothering the man."

"I only answer what he asks of me."

"And what's that?"

"What I plant."

"That's more than he says to his doctor."

A FEW DAYS LATER, ANDREW Lutyen offered a garbled confession that surprised Rain. The doctor wanted to do more surgery on his leg. No guarantee on the outcome, other than he might have less pain and only a small limp. He did not sound enthusiastic.

Rain pulled his booted feet from the sucking ground. Last evening's showers had turned the earth to hungry mud. He'd appear rude if he didn't acknowledge the major.

"Why not, sir?"

"They'll have to send me home."

"Good news."

A long exhale of smoke. "Where's your home, soldier?"

Rain wanted to say, *Bon Sauveur, when the morning mist lets go and the branches steam at dawn,* but the major looked to be a man's man. Instead, Rain picked up his spade and dug.

RAIN LIKED TO GET INTO the gardens before anyone else awoke, when the grounds were wet from night rain or morning dew, and horses lined up through the gate waiting for their drivers to unload their deliveries. He hoped that maybe he'd see Lily. He wanted to tell her about the hummingbirds he'd seen sipping from the yellow and white freesia, how the air nearby was thick with their perfume. But mostly he hid, wanting to spare her his face, now bereft of bandages.

"You're up early," said the major.

Rain hadn't noticed the man against the porch column. The officer wore his tunic, but his shirt was open at the collar.

"I like to get an early start on the day."

Lutyen fumbled in his breast pocket for a cigarette. "Yes, well, all days here are the same."

The man dropped his smoke. "Christ."

"Let me, sir—"

"I'm not a fucking invalid."

The officer placed one crutch against the column and leaned on the other as he bent down, but it happened that he placed his weight on his back leg, and with a groan, fell forward off the porch.

Rain tried to help, but Lutyen would have none at it. He flailed angrily at the turf, pounding it with his fist.

"Please, sir, let me help."

The officer was a solid man and worked to shake himself free of Rain's grasp. He might have succeeded if not for the other pair of hands that tried to hold the major's arm, so close as to almost be touching her skin to his lips. With his fist, the major clocked Lily in the face.

"Jesus Christ." Breathing hard, the officer finally stopped struggling.

Lily, sitting back, pulled her skirts about her knees, and brushed back her hair.

"Oh, it's you," she said when she got a look at Rain.

In the flickering gaze of her gentle pity, any dreams he had for life beyond Bon Sauveur wilted and fell apart, tumbling gently to the ground like the petals in the apple blossom squall in the churchyard.

"Let's get you up, sir," said Rain.

When the major was again standing on the porch and grudgingly accepted his crutches, he bowed slightly to Lily. "You will forgive me, miss."

Major Lutyen then hobbled inside.

"Poor man," she said.

"He'll be all right."

"No, I mean you."

Rain committed to memory her parted lips, the space between her front teeth, the wildness of her eyes as she squeezed through the gates, then ran into the street. Somehow, in all that had happened, she clutched the handful of freesia he'd picked for her and held them to her nose.

THE MAJOR WAS WAITING NEXT MORNING, only now Rain was annoyed. These precious moments before the other men came out to labour alongside him were his. Did the major expect to be out here every day? Probing with questions, wrapped in self-pity, then no doubt swanning back to some county estate to *recover*.

"What's your name, soldier?" the major asked.

"No memory, sir."

"Ah, one of the lucky few, then. What do they call you?"

"The doctor says I was most likely a private," said Rain.

"That young thing yesterday, you know her name?"

"Lily, sir."

"English, I think?"

"London, I hear, sir."

"Her family?"

"Gone, now, sir. So she says."

Major Lutyen nodded. "She strikes me as one of those free-spirited girls you hear about these days."

Rain hadn't heard the term, and he sure didn't care for the tone the officer used. Free-spirited made her sound like a bad girl. A suffragette. Or worse. One of those women with red cheeks and no shame he'd seen on furlough in Paris. Lily did what she did to survive. Many could fault that, but not Rain.

"I believe my behaviour may have been unbecoming," said the major with a bit of a smile.

"IT'S COME ACROSS THE WIRE that Germany wants terms," the doctor told Rain as they walked by the sanatorium chapel where wisteria wrapped and crawled up the steeple.

Dripping, languid clusters of blooms buzzed with honeybees and buried the wall under a purple cascade that swayed back and forth in the afternoon breeze.

"What does that mean?"

The doctor paused in disbelief. "War'll be over, private. The nuns get Bon Sauveur back. We go home."

"Where will I go?"

"Let's not worry about that today. When you came here, I said I'd help you. I'm not leaving with work undone."

The gravel crunched softly under the doctor as he walked away, then looked back. "Oh, but I did want to thank you."

"No need, sir. You were right about men helping me in the gardens. We're making progress."

"Not that. Major Lutyen. He's going ahead with the surgery. I thought you knew."

Rain did not.

"Really? That's odd. When I asked the major why he'd changed his mind, he laughed and said a garden gnome talked him into it. I assumed he was referring to you."

♦♦♦

OCTOBER SENT GOLD AND BROWN leaves tumbling and scratching across the cobbles where they tangled amongst boxwood and shuddering heather. Water dripped through years of neglect into buckets placed in drafty halls.

Lily was the one to tell Rain that Major Lutyen's surgery had been a success. Most of the shrapnel was removed from the leg and the surgeon expected, after a period of recovery, that the officer would again walk without a cane, and possibly only a barely noticeable limp. After a few days in bed, and several more in a wheelchair, Lutyen could begin to rebuild his leg muscles.

"And I'm helping him," Lily said, fighting with a tight-fitting pair of tattered gloves. Rain couldn't find a delicate way of saying that'd only happen over Sister Wicks's dead body. Her dress was new, Rain noticed, at least new to her. Faded blue with faded red roses. Just like one a young woman wore a few days ago, come to the hospital with her mother.

"Most of the sisters are sick in bed, so they even let *me* help. Why not help myself too? I heard Doctor Elliott say the sickness comes from Spain. Everyone's getting it."

Rain didn't think that Lily walking the major, old enough to be her father, up and down the halls was very proper, but he didn't say and later he wished he had.

The gardens needed to be put to rest for the coming winter. Bulbs needed to be planted. The days were getting short. Winter, and death, catches fools unprepared, the old gardener once said. Before the last soldiers were well enough to travel, Doctor Elliott was bound to return to the question of Rain.

MAJOR LUTYEN'S SURGERY WAS THE last the army performed at Bon Sauveur. Lily was now helping in the wards, as were other women from the town, holding feverish heads over enamel bowls to catch vomit, wiping away sweat, emptying bedpans brimming with watery excrement. When able, they stole a few hard-won minutes to rest in the tiny chapel with stained-glass lambs and crosses and bleeding hearts twinkling in the altar candlelight. The place was off limits, but no one prayed anymore or gave a shit about the rules.

Lily leaned back, her head against the pew, exhaling weariness with every breath. It was the first cigarette Rain saw her smoke. The tobacco smelled like Lutyen's. Her cloth mask lay loose about her chin and tangled in a dull gold locket he'd not seen before. No one knew why some people got sick and others didn't. Rain didn't care. Only wanted to lean over and touch his lips to hers.

"Some of them bleed from their mouths and nose," Lily whispered. "Turn purple just before they die."


IF DOCTOR ELLIOTT DIED, THEN maybe no one would ever come for Rain. He hastily mumbled an Act of Contrition, at least what he remembered of it, just in case the God of his youth wasn't quite finished tormenting His creation. Doctor Elliott, who might have escaped the influenza had he not stayed in France to keep a promise to Rain, who never wore collars or ties, whose coat was often stained and whose fiery hair was unkempt. He slept where he could find a bed in the wards. Four years away from America and never managed to speak a word of French without that twanging accent of his, but none of it mattered to the hundreds of people of Caen who respectfully crammed the church to say goodbye when he died. Nor did it matter to Rain, who was certain his careless wish had rubbed another hole into his chalk soul.

STRETCHERS OF GROANING AND FEVERISH bodies clogged the halls and the floors of the refectory. Even the abandoned cells in the cellars where common incurables had once gone mad, scarred with syphilis and the ancient mercury cure, were fitted with metal folding cots over latrine drains still stinking of urine. No one cheered the signing of the Armistice.

. Rain joined the others in the hospital, including Lily and anyone able to stand, but to him fell the emptying of bedpans, the paisley swirls in the viscous brown contents making him puke dryly into already overflowing basins. Sleep, when he could get it, came curled in a corner when his legs no longer moved, and his muscles ached, and he feared that he too had finally caught the deadly influenza. No one worried about his rest or if he found something to eat, not when there was another bucket to empty, vomit to be mopped, when wood was needed for a fire growing cold. All this Rain did because if Lily could stand it, so could he. If he was lucky, from across a crowded room, her face flushed hot and wet, Rain might get a quick wave.

"The spruce tree in the entrance hall, is it from you?" she asked.

"Bit of Christmas, for the children. I thought it might make them feel better."

Lily wiped her forehead with her arm. "Sad one for most of them, I think. Lots of them are alone now."

"And you?"

She shrugged. "I don't mind. Might even get another dress."

When Rain thought he could no longer stand the stench of bodies soiling themselves, could not stomach the bile on the floors, could not collect another corpse for burial, he escaped outside into a bitter December. He'd rather think about what the frozen beds of mud and naked branches would bring forth in the spring, when this strange malady passed, this sickness that came so quickly, took the strongest, and left the dead looking startled that the body could survive four years of war, only to succumb to a virus in hours.

Down the gravel walk to the gates, unlocked now with the constant wagons pulling into the courtyard, the carrying off of the sick, the bringing out of the dead, and there was no one to man them. No one to oppose him. Rusting, they squeaked as he stepped out into the winding streets, empty of people, windows shuttered.

He was free for the first time since he'd lied about his age and signed up to fight. By the doors, trellises and clay pots filled with the brittle remains of summer, eaten away by frost. Rowboats tied along the canal bounced against tight waves cropped with slim tips of white. A dog eyed him hungrily. Any one of those boats could take him down the waterway and to the coast. From there, England. No one to know. No one to stop him, and yet, no place to go.

No, there was only here and the need for him back at the hospital. A debt, penance perhaps, to a kindly doctor, and Lily, the girl he tried to guard his heart against though she already owned it.

Rain had walked as far as l'église Saint-Pierre, stern reminder of a God who would most certainly hold him accountable. Under its black-washed spire and great eye of a window, a scattering of stalls offered meagre piles of potatoes and beets and onions, watched over by desiccated women with clicking needles, and weary white-bearded men who blinked at the sky. Behind the seller of well-thumbed books, a half-done, one-eyed Madonna wrapped in a sky-blue headdress was rendered in chalk.

"Beautiful."

The bookseller wiped away the drop pooling at the end of his nose and glanced over his shoulder when he noticed Rain looking at the unfinished Virgin.

"Ah, Anglais, ignore her, she does not listen. I started her when my wife took ill. Forty-seven years we had. Almost." He nodded with a bit of a grimace. "You are not from here?"

"No, Bon Sauveur."

"Ah, yes, many foreigners at the hospital."

"You draw well."

"You think so, young fellow?"

The bookseller lifted a leather satchel and dropped it on the table. It was full of coloured chalk.

"No more. I hoped honouring the Virgin would save my dear wife's life. Now I've no heart to finish her. The priests, they lie to us, I think. I pray now only to join my Beatrice."

"What will you do with the chalk?"

"You want it? Take it. One less thing for me to carry."


IN THE GARDENER'S SHED, BY lantern, Rain emptied the leather satchel. Eight different greens, three reds, four shades of pink, as well as blue and indigo and turquoise, some yellows and oranges, and a purple.

Rain, remembering sketching lessons dedicated to carved stone, and marble faces, and blossoms, looked below the surface.

HE REMOVED ALL THE HANGING rakes and hoes, baskets and burlap sacking, clearing everything out of the old gardener's cramped stone shed. He swept cobwebs, brought down the ancient hornets' nest in the rafters. Pulled the heavy, ornately carved armoire with shelves of jars of rusting nails away from the wall and lay it on the floor. The hole where pigeons came in to roost he nailed shut with old wooden shutters. Rain hung a lantern from the ceiling, and placed others in each corner.

He began by tracing his designs first on paper, then on the inside of the stone walls. He drew when he could, often only at night, all through the night, so that he began his duties in the wards with barely an hour or two of sleep. With dawn, what feeble warmth the lanterns offered was gone and Rain bounced on his feet, blowing into his hands, his breath heavy and white before him.

Laying the outline was painstaking work. Each stroke had to be perfect. Rain's raw hands throbbed from the exertion. Still, he smiled to do it, though it felt as if his mouth was not his. He smiled as red and yellow-tinged chalk hibiscus, and lavender, canopied with minty chestnut trees, and baskets spilling over with pink mayflowers, spread over the walls, surrounding the blue cornflower in the centre.

By Christmas Eve, all was ready. Meeting Lily in the refectory, he pulled her aside and quietly asked if she could come to the gardener's hut. He guessed she was planning to attend the service in the chapel that evening, to be near her major, so Rain would be waiting for her on her way back.

"A present? For me?" Lily touched his arm, added that she couldn't wait.

Rain continued to mop the floor in the entrance hall, still feeling her touch on his skin, watching Lily join the other women from Caen who'd volunteered to nurse the sick pull on hats and coats for the short walk to Bon Sauveur's chapel. A grim Christmas service it would be. As soon as they were gone, Rain dropped the mop and ran to the shed. He had an hour or so to touch up his chalk garden, make sure everything was perfect.

When the bells rang at the ending of the service Rain blew into his hands, then shoved them under his arms, but nothing stopped them, him, from shaking. He wasn't fool enough to think she'd ever love him, and besides, all that he'd thought love meant had no place in this world now, but this memory of summer they could share. Perhaps it was as close to love as Rain would get.

THE CHRISTMAS EVE BELLS PEELING across the ancient city became the bells of Christmas Day. The oil in the lanterns had grown low. Rain turned all but one down to save what remained. Outside the door of the hut, a light snow fell, uncommitted, soon ending as quickly as it began. He sat huddled, back against the wall.

*Idiot.*

He kicked the lantern and the light went out.

RAIN WOKE TO RAPID KNOCKING on the door. Standing, he winced at the stiff shoulder that had propped him against the icy wall through the night. The window allowed an orange line of dawn, a thin crust of snow lay on its sill. Christmas morning promised to be warm under the sun, but Lily already looked flushed.

"Thank goodness you're here!"

Her coat was buttoned to her neck. Her hair was hastily pinned under her hat and beginning already to rebel. She gripped a suitcase and her lips were very red.

"Major Lutyen...my Andrew...he's waiting by the gate! Home to England, can you believe it? Aren't you just the happiest for me?"

Dawn was warm against the snow in the eaves. If Lily remained, she'd get wet.

"And he says he'll marry me!" She reached to kiss him briefly, but then thought better of it, touched his cheek with warm fingers, and was gone.

Rain watched her hurry across the path he had made for her to where the major was waiting outside the gate. Her footprints made little holes in the thin layer of white. Lutyen tossed his cigarette, saluted victoriously, and climbed into the automobile as the snow melted and dripped through the roof of the shed, streaking the chalk-covered walls. As the automobile sped away, Rain remembered to breathe.

*Malus domestica*

# 1925

Nothing could save the apple tree at Bon Sauveur. Winter had been too hard. The first cut of the trunk showered Rain with twigs. He wiped his eyes with the back of his hand and tightened his grip on the axe. The tree fought the next blow, holding the blade deep in the wound. Drops from the coming storm broke hard and fast against the flat stones, and soon his wet clothes clung to him as he struggled to pull the axe free. Rain struck again, oblivious to the purring Phantom easing under the sanatorium's gate and pulling alongside the chapel's hedge of boxwood, wrapped with chicken wire to ward off hungry rabbits. The tree rattled as the trunk split and tore loudly, and the heavy canopy tipped toward the ground, bouncing on the grass.

A large black umbrella bloomed from the open driver's side door. Rain watched his own face reflected in the car's buffed, drop-spotted lacquer as the driver opened the rear door, from which the passenger, his striped suit impeccably tailored, saluted Rain with two fingers.

"Major?"

"Civilian now, private." Peace clearly agreed with Andrew Lutyen. Are you just going to stand there?"

"He's wet," the driver observed, glancing at Rain's overalls and rubber galoshes, all muddy.

"Quite right."

Rain was oblivious to the water dripping off the brim of his hat.

"I see that I've surprised you," said Lutyen.

Patients, the ones who lived, rarely came back. Certainly not to see Rain.

"But did you know that you're the talk of Paris, my friend? The self-taught gardener with the mysterious past who's turned the grounds of a somewhat unsavoury institution into a place where families frolic on holidays. Quite a legend. Of course I told Lily that it couldn't be you. You'd be long gone from Bon Sauveur. Yet here you are."

*Lily?*

"Don't say you've forgotten her. She won't like that."

"No, I haven't forgotten." *Not for a moment.*

"Good, because she simply won't take no for an answer." Lutyen leaned forward, looked about the grounds. "Christ, man, it's true what they say about you. What you do with colour is breathtaking. Not the Bon Sauveur I remember. Are the grounds always like this?"

"Not always so wet."

"Ha! Come work for me."

"Sir?"

"I've done all right. Better than all right. Got a knack for the markets. But Lily and I are tired of London. We want something quiet, so I've purchased a spot up north. Nearly a ruin if you listen to Lily, but it's got a garden, or it did, once. What do you say, man? Come work your magic for me."

Rain glanced at the driver.

"What are you looking at him for? You don't need his permission."

How could a man like Andrew Lutyen understand? *I'm happy here* really meant that he had got used to being alone, preferring the *idea* of something...someone...Lily, to the real thing. A dream never disappointed. Besides, here mostly no one much cared about his face anymore, and so days would go by when he didn't either. In the evenings, the nuns gave him access to their library so long as he kept mud off the carpet, and he leafed through André Le Nôtre's sketches for the gardens at Versailles, Capability Brown's notes for the grounds at Blenheim, books amassed over the years from lords and earls and dukes who'd come for venereal treatment along with their personal libraries, though most had not left. His favourite was a nineteenth-century folio by Joseph Banks from his journeys through the Antipodes with gloriously detailed watercolours of eucalyptus—those massive self-pruning gum trees. It was his personal Oxford, Rain often mused, though many of these texts only validated the lessons he had first learned from the old gardener a decade ago.

"You live in a shed and those parsimonious nuns pay you nothing. Don't deny it. I've done my homework. I'll pay you a generous salary and provide a cottage, a decent cottage."

What was the promise of money? Rain made enough, quietly selling off peony blossoms for a franc, wrapped in newspaper for the women of Caen to put on the graves of the war dead. There were always more graves than peonies, which meant he had enough to purchase pens and sketching paper. As for his home, the shed had a stove now, and Rain was more than welcome to take meals in the refectory. Surely Lutyen wanted a real gardener, an artist who'd studied his craft, had certificates, cut his teeth in service on some fine English estate.

"Lily wants you." Lutyen indicated with a nod that the driver should get back behind the wheel. "You'll change your mind and when you do, I'll arrange passage for you to Portsmouth, and then to London."

Mother Superior sat behind the desk with one hand over her nose. She appeared troubled.

"The Daughters of the Good Saviour shall be sorry to see you go," she said.

Rain, standing in the doorway, clutched his hat, and looked at the floor. Her hasty summons had given him no time to wash off the smell of sheep manure.

"We are grateful for your work here in the gardens."

"I've asked for nothing but to stay—"

"And regrettably, that is no longer possible. It's been brought to my attention that there is some question as to your war record. You are not who you say you are."

"I don't know who I am. Was."

"People in Caen have not forgotten what...who they sacrificed in the war. If it got out that you were hiding from some, trouble, here at Bon Sauveur, it's a scandal the hospital, and Our Mother the Church, cannot have."

"Please—"

Mother Superior rose and not quite offered her hand. "If it's any consolation, I always thought your work here was a labour of love. No, an act of love. God will be pleased, my son."

Rain stayed in London long enough to be fitted for the suit of clothes Lutyen insisted upon him having. It was his first since the army, uneasily measured in front of the mirror where there was no turning away from this bespoke torment: the almost bald and round reflection, being asked painfully private questions like on what side did the gentleman dress and what fabric did sir prefer for his undergarments. Bolts of wool and linen and cotton blocked most of the high street window, save for a brief gap through which

Rain watched women with shortened skirts hurry by and wondered if the war and its legacy of shortages had caused the rising of hems.

"Giving 'em the vote is what's done it," said the tailor kneeling about Rain's trousers, wearing measuring tapes like a scarf, and squinting despite his thick glasses as he inserted pins into delicate chalk markings.

The face staring back at Rain from the mirror would have made him grimace if he could. Doctor Elliott was right. Rain was growing into it, but that was little comfort. His nose, no longer an onion, remained fat, with a nod to the right. His lips were fleshy, the bottom one protruding so that his mouth didn't close properly. Scars, although fading, laced his forehead and face, and his cheeks, where they'd been sewn back together, drew up at the corners of his mouth in a perpetual clown smile.

"A right gentleman's suit, sir."

*Sewing feathers on a gourd*, thought Rain, who longed for his comfortable patched overalls now in a bin out back of the shop.

Lutyen's driver had met Rain at the York train station. The same expressionless man Rain was to now call Marshall, with mutton chop whiskers, whose buttons were as polished as the lacquer on the major's automobile. Marshall wasn't one to chat. Nor did he think he had to open the door for Rain and his suitcase. The drive was to take about one hour, Marshall said, as they moved out of the shadow of York Minster, which Rain thought much finer than Caen's l'église Saint-Pierre, past stone houses with drab slate roofs jostling for pride of place on narrow streets, and into a countryside of recumbent blackened-stone churches casting their judgment over fields of tombstones surrounded by piled rocks fencing off verdant fields and copses of green mulberry and oak.

The wiper on the windscreen swished back and forth against the pervasive damp, across the low skies and emerald squares. The memory of Bon Sauveur's beds of eager tulips, crowding yearly out of the ground, bobbing under the sun's benediction, faded with each passing milestone. So too the dripping wisteria turning the chapel wall into a waterfall of purple, the avenues of peonies, their heavy heads of white and pink genuflecting against the gravel path, and the cherry blossom petals, carried on the wind across the courtyard, chased by the town's children. England was wet wind and low dark clouds, a winding driveway and towering, shaggy elms clutching for the top of the passing Phantom. England was Lily.

Marshall's eye caught him through the mirror. "I'll pull over if you're going to be ill."

RAIN UNFOLDED HIMSELF from THE tight confines of the back seat, pulling his suitcase roughly out behind him just in time before Marshall drove away and left him, standing without ceremony on the cobbled driveway clogged with wagons and vans and men unloading what appeared to be an unending stream of newly minted copper pipes. He looked up at the high facade of Lutyen's purchase—a brutish, two-storey Georgian house of canary sandstone now blackened by York's sooty mist. His gaze was drawn upward by the portico awkwardly held in place by towering Corinthian columns, and he was reminded of the tweed suit he wore: someone else's idea, added, incongruously, at a later date.

"Watch where you step!" shouted a glazier clinging from a ladder as he replaced the pane of glass in a long rectangular window. Roofers scrambled about the upper storey, yelled ho!, and tossed broken tiles about Rain's feet. No one seemed to know where the major was, or where Rain was to go.

Stepping gingerly over paint-speckled tarpaulins and dodging trades, Rain made his way into the hall. Grand or stately it may have once been, but now its air was sweet with the floury odours of new plaster and freshly hung wallpaper, not yet realized as its latest incarnation. Framed staircases climbed both sides of the great room, laden with men who ripped out their rotted supports and hammered polished treads back in their place. Here and there, men perched on scaffolding, wrestling with delicate, decaying ceiling moulding and cursing loudly. And conducting all this from an old door slung across a pair of sawhorses, and covered with sketches and drawings, was Major Lutyen, the man and the master.

"I give you a week's vacation and yet here you are! You do know what a vacation is?" Despite this greeting Lutyen's handshake was welcoming. And just like that, all Rain's well-rehearsed demands—namely, that the major defend his role in making him leave Bon Sauveur—vanished.

"At least my tailor made you look like a gentleman," said Lutyen, glancing over the cut of the uncomfortable tweed. "So, private, welcome to Walling. Quick, first impression. Be honest."

Looking about at all this room and promise, Rain recalled the dirty-faced boy he'd once been. This house was a thing he could only dream about then as he lay wedged into an iron-framed bed with two others every night.

"A place for a family" was all he could manage.

Lutyen turned back to his drawings and Rain wondered if he'd offended the man. "Hungry for money is what this place is," he replied. "Every day I hear a wall will buckle, a floor will collapse. I'll have rebuilt the entire house by time I'm done. But, if it's what my *dear* wife wants, she shall have it. Anything to make her comfortable."

"Is...she here?"

"In London for the season with Evie, my sister. Quite the dragon, my dear sister. Be thankful she's not here. She stays in that town-house I bought her, and I'm not expected to visit. We like it that way."

Rain glanced over the plans. He could see nothing of the gardens.

"Oh, you'll have plenty to keep you busy, private. If you're not too tired from your journey, come with me."

He led Rain to the far end of the great hall, and outside, into the courtyard: a large rectangle bordered on all sides by the great hall, the east and west wings, and a low black-shingled barn that looked to have endured centuries of royal back-and-forth before becoming a storage shed for hay and carriages. The courtyard was a mess of broken paving stones pitched crooked by encroaching nature, cracked stone urns, and waiting piles of replacement tiles for the roof.

Lutyen pointed with his cane to the upper storeys of the east and west wings. Only the east looked habitable.

"The bedchambers will be up there and there, but I can't have my guests looking out on this diabolical madness, nor that blight of a barn. Rafters are full of filthy birds. You'll see that it comes down. But first," he pointed again to each wing in turn, "we replace those upper windows with doors. Then we run a balcony the length of each wing. Down here," he pointed to the ground in front of them, "we'll put in a swimming pool. Lily loves to swim, but it'll have to be heated before she'll dip a toe into it. Got myself a real piece of art for the fountain."

Lutyen leaned on his cane heavily as he walked Rain about the courtyard. "Damn leg!" He stopped in pain, to tap his thigh. "As if that bloody war didn't take enough. Can you believe I fell on it? Riding accident, after all that business I went through in France. At least I know when the weather's going to turn. Ha! But enough of woe. Let's get you settled. I've set you up in one of the cottages, not far."

They passed back through the cacophony of the great hall and out into the driveway where Lutyen waved over one of his men.

"This fellow will take you to your cottage, private. I'm a man of my word. You'll be smothered in pillows and quilts. The former tenant brought in the plumbing, and after the main house here gets electrics, I'll see that a wire is run out to you. But don't get too comfortable. You'll want to get started looking around, I expect."

"The courtyard?"

"Good heavens, man, yes, to start with, but that's not why you're here. Walling has seven thousand acres! Make it a garden my wife will never want to leave."

THE WELL-WORN WOOD of the table was smooth, almost buttery. The kitchen with its stone hearth would be warm. The cottage also had a front room with a horsehair sofa, and two rooms upstairs. More space than he'd ever known, just for him. Most likely, he'd never use most of it. The previous tenant had painted the cottage door and window frames a deep burgundy, perfect against the black-stained sandstone walls that stood in the middle of thousands of acres he would make bloom for her.

Lutyen offered Rain the use of one of the estate's Austins, but the roads were pitted and overgrown and Rain preferred to head out on foot before dawn with his hat and his old oilskin coat, a canteen and some bread rolls in his rucksack, along with pads of paper, pencils, and a knife. There was nothing like the squeak of grass breaking against his boots at dawn, watching the clouds being torn off distant hills, looking out over vales carpeted in heather.

Walling was covered in pathways—some nettle-choked trails, others paved with stones smoothed by centuries of hikers, or if he believed Lutyen, legions of Romans. A fast-moving river, a half a mile or so from the house and easily seen if not for the old barn in the courtyard, caught itself in pool-like bends around the bone-white remnants of a sunken forest. Rain even found the overgrown ruin of a domed Georgian folly. Nearby, the dressed stones of an embankment, overgrown with bilberries, marked where once this structure's reflection had shimmered in an ornamental pool.

OVER THE SUMMER, the house's outer walls were scrubbed to yellow. Gaping holes became windows, and freshly cut wood and smoothed plaster were kept dry by the patched roof. The copper pipes were installed, and most of the workmen's wagons were gone, replaced by moving vans delivering chairs and sofas, heavy marble-topped tables, and giant glazed urns filled with tree-sized palms. At least once a week Rain ended his daily walk with a visit to the courtyard, with its newly completed swimming pool, not only to imagine what he would create there, but to see the progress inside the house now that the walls had been hung with paper and the artisans had taken down their scaffolds from the intricately retouched mouldings. By last sun, he'd make his way the mile or so along the grass path to his cottage, happy to be tired, hopeful for dreams that did not include another man's wife.

On his kitchen table, already covered with open books and sketches, Rain dropped his notepad. Made a better worktable anyhow. Sitting there alone to eat a meal made the cottage feel more empty than it already did, and besides, he ate what he cooked standing over the pot, or tore from a loaf. Same thing for the bedroom upstairs, although the bed was large and he did give it a bounce. The horsehair sofa in the front room, with a blanket, looked to be comfortable enough, only today, she was sitting on it.

Lily's hair was bobbed now, to just below the ear. It shimmered like platinum, straight and glossy, and held in place with a black velvet band and a diamond pin. Her pale arm stretched along the back of the sofa as she exhaled the smoke from her cigrarette.

"Have I frightened you, my darling thing?"

The songbirds outside seemed to be silent. Her words sounded hard and staged, as if she had rehearsed them in front of a mirror, thinking it best to emphasize some words over others, without understanding why.

"Yes," he said, maddened by his boyish squeak.

She stood and opened her arms. "Oh, come here and hug me like a brother."

Rain's boots clunked heavily on the wood floor, splattering field mud. Lily didn't seem to care. She put her arms around him and laughed a little at the sound of the breath catching in his throat.

"You look...." She cocked her head at him. "Not as bad as I remember. I can't believe you stayed in that dreadful place all these years! You must thank me for rescuing you."

"It wasn't so bad." Rain inelegantly pulled off his boots.

"You've been well? Andrew's been kind? He can be...brutish at times."

Rain nodded.

"Good. I couldn't stand you being treated poorly. It'd be like kicking a puppy. Now, come." She patted the sofa.

Rain tried to cover the hole in his sock with his other foot as Lily tossed her cigarette into the hearth, then took his hand.

"You got your wish," he noticed.

Lily held up her hand and looked at the diamond on her ring finger long and hard, as if it were old and needed polishing, or remembering what it was for. "Yes, so it seems."

She dropped her hand. "But I'm so glad you came. I knew you would."

"Your husband didn't give me a choice."

She grinned. "Was he devious? Andrew *does* like to get what he wants! But aren't you glad to be here? Say you are."

Rain nodded unsurely, flummoxed by this bold and worldly version of the girl of his dreams—girl no longer—who was already reaching for a new cigarette and offering him the opportunity to light it.

"Good. Because what I need is a friend. Oh, I do have lots, of course, but not a *real* one like you."

Her lips were very red.

"Andrew says it's your job to make me happy here."

"I thought you wanted to be away from London?"

"Did Andrew tell you that? He would, wouldn't he." Lily jumped up. "What have you got to drink?"

Rain didn't think anything.

"I'll send for some whiskey to be brought down from the house. A whole case full. You don't mind me coming down here to drink, do you?" She was at the window now. "My idea to give you this cottage. You can't see it from the house." She let the curtain drop. "You'd do anything for me, wouldn't you? Yes, I know you would, so I can tell you this." The cigarette between her fingers smouldered, untouched by her lips. "I'm a prisoner here. Chained by my husband."

Whatever else Rain thought about Lutyen, he was sure the man loved his wife.

"Have you ever made a mistake?"

Lily didn't wait for a reply as she went to the kitchen and opened cupboards. "Are you sure you've got nothing to drink?" she called back.

Rain followed, offering to try his hand at tea. Perhaps there was some in a tin on the kitchen shelf, though he had never really mastered brewing it.

Lily sighed, or groaned. It was hard to know. She didn't want tea, or to be a wife. She wanted to have fun.

"Maybe even have a career. Make my own money. Lots of women do now. I've even thought about being in the pictures. I could be the next Nina Vanna."

Rain had never seen a film.

"Let's go to York, then. Make a day of it, just us. Can you drive? Doesn't matter. I can, as long as no one else is on the road."

Her words were coming at him so quickly.

"The major?"

"What about him? It's not like he has anything to worry about when I'm with you, is it? Although I do love you," she added, sounding weary, as if the sentiment was demanded of her. "Glad to have me out of his way, truth be told. Says he's fixing up that house for me, but God forbid I make any suggestions! Doesn't want me around to see the bars going up on the windows." She grabbed Rain's palm and tapped the last bit of cigarette ash onto it. "One day I'll divorce him. Won't that just be a scandal. Lots of people are doing it now. Quite common. And I could, you know, because of what the war did to him...because he can't...." Lily tucked back a curve of hair that had fallen to the corner of her mouth.

Rain held his breath. He wanted nothing to spoil this moment, including a clumsy word from himself.

"Now, my darling thing, the real reason I'm here is Saturday. Have you evening clothes?"

"No, why?"

"For the party, of course. Andrew wants to show off my new jail. I won't have a single friend there, so say you'll come. You must."

"I've just my tweed."

"That won't do." Lily looked Rain over. "You're bigger than I remember. One of Andrew's old ones is out of the question. I'll send over a tailor."

AUTOMOBILES BEGAN ARRIVING in the late afternoon and by evening, a solid glow of headlights snaked along the road from York. Marshall took his post in a field near the house and waved the drivers into long rows with the help of an electric torch. From there, guests giggled their way towards the lights and music on a boardwalk zigzagging over the grass, built to save the many pairs of satin pumps from the evening dew.

Rain hurried past Marshall without a word of greeting, trussed up in the evening suit the tailor had dropped off that morning, his shoes thumping on the wooden path. No telling if his collar was crooked or if he had got the bowtie right. Rain hadn't stayed in front of the mirror long enough to check. Luckily it was dark and Marshall seemed incapable of more than one facial expression anyway, so Rain couldn't be sure what the driver thought about the gardener being dolled up as a guest.

Every window blazed at Walling, and torches burned atop stone urns along the driveway. Electric bulbs even hung from trees and were threaded through the low shrubs and bushes. Lutyen was a man of his word, and already posts had been erected to run a wire from the main house to Rain's cottage. A telephone would be next. If she couldn't be in London, Lily said, she could at least talk to London. But tonight, all of London looked to be at Walling.

Rain could hear the music wailing—the distant saxophone shrill, almost frantic—long before he stepped into the great hall, where even the walls seemed to pulse, much to the apparent displeasure of a tall, thin woman, descending one of the newly rebuilt staircases. Wrapped in layers of gathered and tucked tulle, her black hair so short and shining it looked like polish upon her skull, she reminded Rain of the formidable bow of the Portsmouth ferry slowly easing into dock.

"And you are?" she asked, as if the day had been one long weary ordeal after another.

"The gardener," he said foolishly, immediately wishing he hadn't.

Rain feared that her up-and-down gaze meant he'd left something unbuttoned.

"My brother and his wife have no more sense than the playthings they associate with. I said they should get the man from Montacute House to do the gardens here, a *real* gardener. Instead, here *you* are." Evie Lutyen's shoes clicked on the marble floor as she landed in front of him. "But what do I know about such things, as I'm often reminded."

Rain would rather feel foolishly out of place joining the other guests heading to the courtyard than stand under this woman's terrifying stare any longer.

"Where do you think you're going?"

"Lily...she asked me to come."

Evie nodded to the door tucked discretely under the sweep of the opposite staircase. "It's Mrs. Lutyen to you, young man, and that way to the kitchen."

No, he was a guest. Hadn't Lily invited him, arranged for this dreadful suit?

The crowd outside cheered.

All those beautiful people.

What had he been thinking?

Evie could smile, like she was doing now, because maybe the war had turned the world upside-down and a besotted brother could make a silly harlot his wife, but someone still had to hold firm on propriety and keep the foolish gardener from waltzing through the front door as if he were their equal.

She was right. He was an idiot. Men like Andrew Lutyen, women like Lily, did not make a guest out of help. He was properly attired and ready to serve.

On the other side of the door and down a long narrow hall, Rain entered a steaming kitchen filled with shouting red-faced women in bandannas, and countertops piled with glasses.

"You're late," said a tall thin man who sounded like he talked through his nose. He pulled Rain close and retied the bowtie. "A bit of rough, but if you can carry something you'll do." He shoved a silver tray of crackers covered in bits of salmon into Rain's hands. "When it's empty, come and get another."

With a final shove against his back, Rain found himself pressed through another door and into the crush of guests in the courtyard.

Lights strung on ropes from the roof lit the now-filled pool and made the water glitter. Around it, sweating dancers convulsed in a frenzied mix of shimmies, rolling shoulders, and neck jerks, offered as adulation to, or perhaps enslaved by, the eight-man orchestra playing frantically on the new balcony that ran the length of the west wing. A man embracing a large round microphone sang about having yes! yes! in your eyes and counting girls instead of sheep. A girl with rouge on her cheeks held a drink high as she ran to the end of the diving board and bounded and twirled. Her stockings sparkled under the lights and the rows of tassels on her very short dress bounded up and down—more so still when a trio of young fellows joined her, whooping and laughing and bouncing with the music until the board cracked and split, and they splashed into the pool, dousing others nearby. The girl thrashed about in the water, screaming that she couldn't swim, the glass still in her hand, but no one was bothered. The musicians played faster.

A young man with round spectacles clasped Rain's shoulder and waved an empty glass.

"Gin," he demanded, "not a tray of stinkin' fish crackers." He must have gin and it was too far to walk back to his automobile for the stash he had in his trunk, and was the rumour true? Was the pool filled with vodka? He'd heard it was filled with vodka. Time for a dip. Then he was swept into the tide of dancers circling the water. Rain saw the young fellow shortly after when he dove into the pool, came up spitting out water that was not vodka, and inadvertently saved the drowning girl in the tassels that flickered like goldfish.

Rain felt himself in a nightmare. Surely no one would see him leave. He could just put down the tray, walk to the edge of the courtyard, and slip out between the bushes. And on the way back to his cottage, he could strip off his black jacket and tear it to shreds.

"You made it, my darling, and don't you look spiffy," said Lily, drunkenly. "I told Andrew you'd shine up! He said it couldn't be done. We made a bet, shush, don't you know gambling is my new sin. I have many. I collect them. You really must try it. Have you seen him?"

"Who?"

"My husband, silly."

Rain shook his head, wondering why Lily was talking as if she were trying out new words.

"Good. He's a flat tire because I invited a few more people and tonight, tonight I just want to get spifflicated."

"What?"

"Ossified! Drunk, you ninny!"

Lily's long strand of pearls bounced around her silver dress. Her lips were very moist and because of the push of the crowd and the noise, they almost had to touch Rain's face so that he could hear her speak.

"Now come, you must dance with me."

The silver tray of salmon on crackers came between them.

"What are you doing with that?"

"I met your sister-in-law."

"And she made you do this? That cow'll be on the first train to London in the morning."

A woman, shrilly, repeatedly, called her name, adding *dah-ling*.

"Here, put that damn tray down and hold me up."

The air around her was spiced with her scent, a combination of lavender and orange and sweat, as his arms lifted her to look over the crowd and wave. Sliding back down, she pressed her breasts against his face.

"I want that dance. Promise?"

Then she was gone.

EXCEPT FOR THE COUPLES with tongues down each other's throats, the girls' dresses hiked up so the young men could more easily wrap their legs about their waists, and the one fellow who'd had too much to drink and who was now vomiting quite determinedly, no one bothered to cross into the damp grass surrounding the barn. Lutyen found Rain there leaning against the corner, watching the dancing, plotting his escape.

"Not enjoying yourself?"

Rain straightened, pulled down his cuffs.

Lutyen tapped out a cigarette and offered one.

"This is her idea of a few friends over for dinner." Lutyen cupped his lighter to his mouth, then puffed, puffed. "There's a viscount, three lords, a prince from a country that no longer exists, and eighteen members of parliament in that crowd. Just enough to make my sister happy. My wife thinks Evie's screwy, one of the many rather vulgar expressions she's picked up from American magazines, but Lily's no good at running a house like Walling and I want someone who won't rob me blind. I take it you've met my sister?"

Rain nodded.

"Titles are important to her, even if the bloody sods are really here for my free booze, and maybe a tip about the markets. Why aren't you up there dancing?"

Because dancing was for those pretty boys around the pool, either thin or muscular, heads shiny with Brilliantine, preening waistcoats with silver buttons and diamond studs. Athletic men who could easily strip off their jackets and trousers for a boister-ous night swim, then flex themselves on the poolside with an impish grin. Maybe rich, maybe only pretending, but confident their easy swagger and unblemished beauty was beguiling.

"Not my thing either, but cheer up, party can't last forever." Lutyen rubbed his gamey leg knowingly. "Storm coming."

Except that there was no hint of weather between them and the stars.

Lutyen tossed the end of his cigarette hissing into the wet grass. "I'm tired of looking at the dirt around the pool. How are the plans coming for my garden?"

Notes, a few sketches, the overall plan elusive, but Lutyen wasn't listening. A polite inquiry not intended to be replied to. The music may have been loud, but Rain didn't think the man was listening to that either.

"She'll do this again tomorrow, if I let her. A different party every night. She never seems to tire of the novelty." Lutyen smiled with great effort and clapped Rain on the shoulder. "I don't envy you. Making her a garden that doesn't bore her after a day won't be easy."

SHORTLY BEFORE DAWN RAIN made his way to his cottage by way of the wooden footpath, under the squeak and flit of bats. The weather Lutyen had felt in his leg blew in dark and quickly, threatening already drooping feathered headbands and tugging at fur-tipped wraps. Marshall, still at his post, was trying to wave the cars out of the field in single file, but no one wanted to wait or stop honking their horns. Two men walked ahead of Rain, one with a girl slung lifelessly over his shoulders. Her ring-covered fingers moved back and forth in rhythm with the fringe on her dress.

Rain reached the cottage just as the heavens broke. He carefully removed his suit and hung it in the wardrobe, where he told the moths to have at it. He hoped never to have to wear it again and that Lily had exhausted the need to include him in Walling's revelries. Morning was already cutting an oblique line across the kitchen when Rain put water on to boil. No expectation of sleep after such a night, and sitting down, he opened his sketchpad to a blank page.

Hers could not be a garden of rose beds or leafy walks. Romantic vistas would make her laugh, but not happily. Lily's garden had to delight her constantly. That delight would make her happy and happiness, as Lutyen believed, was key to keeping Lily at Walling. And Rain near Lily.

The kettle boiled and Rain rose mechanically to make tea that would most surely go cold before he thought to have a sip.

After he filled the pot, he placed it on the table next to a mug. He had been too nervous to eat before the party, and too wary to be caught eating by that Evie. He pulled a tin of crackers out of the cupboard and placed it beside his mug.

The gentle nudge from his employer had not gone amiss, but the blank page in front of Rain reminded him that he had nothing. No ideas, no thoughts, no plans for Lily's garden. Nothing that would amuse her. How could he? Gardens were dictated by the slow movement of seasons, unfolding over weeks and months, even years. Lutyen was losing Lily to a postwar world where nothing but pleasure, pleasure to excess and in the moment, mattered. What Andrew Lutyen really wanted was for Rain to slow down time, to help him hold onto the woman he loved. The woman they loved.

But Rain couldn't see how.

He pulled the empty sketchpad towards him, poured tea into his mug. Sliding the pot away, he pulled the mug closer. Reached for the tin of crackers. He opened it, then closed it and slid it back and forth across the table. Back and forth.

A BLEARY-EYED WOMAN IN AN APRON who found it much too early to smile escorted Rain into the library where he found Lutyen at breakfast, staring blankly at a headline about the nation's coal pit trouble. Through the window, Rain saw his employer's household, the very same people who had attended the guests only a few hours before, wrestling with umbrellas and gathering glasses, mounting ladders and taking down the lights in the wind and rain. A woman's dress, myriad cigarette butts, and a dead seagull floated in the choppy pool water.

"Good heavens, man. Don't you own an umbrella?"

Rain took the chair that was offered and pulled several sheets of paper out of his pocket. "I couldn't sleep."

Lutyen nodded to the woman who had taken up her post in the corner to pour for Rain and remove his wet coat.

"Have you eaten?"

"Not until you see this."

"At least get this coffee into you, man."

"We need a greenhouse. A very big one, because the growing season here is too short. High enough to allow for full-grown trees." Rain pointed to his hand-drawn map of Walling. "There. The lane behind the barn, it'll go behind that rise. But it'll have to be positioned back enough to stay hidden from the main house."

The drawings were hastily but artfully rendered and Rain confessed to knowing even less about building a greenhouse than he believed he knew about gardening, but a greenhouse they needed to realize this mad idea. And the money—

"What are you saying?"

That Lily would never think Walling more than prison. Rain had watched her at the party, heard her laugh, seen her eyes dart with every passing moment from one diversion to the next. If she was to stay willingly, each day had to contain an unexpected new delight, a surprise, the anticipation of an adventure.

"A new garden."

"In a greenhouse? Not quite what I expected."

"Not *in* the greenhouse. We use the plants in the greenhouse to change the garden."

"All well and good, but—"

"Every day."

"What? How?"

"I haven't got all the details worked out. Not entirely. But look."

As Rain explained his drawings, Lutyen's gaze became more intent.

"You are a mad bastard," he said when Rain took a breath and sat back. Then he laughed.

BY MID-AFTERNOON, LUTYEN AND RAIN, and a hungover architect from York who only hours before had swam at Walling as a guest, paced out the foundation of the greenhouse. When complete, they stood back and surveyed the quarter square mile. The architect, arms akimbo, said this could very well be the largest building of glass constructed since the Crystal Palace.

LUTYEN HAD BUSINESS, EXTENSIVE BUSINESS, he said, in New York. Lily would go with him. Evie offered to stay at Walling and make sure the household kept to its routine—and did not help itself to the silver or the fruit preserves. Lutyen worried she'd interfere with the plans for the garden, but surely the house and its people would keep her too occupied to be of any trouble. In the time that they were away, could Rain complete the transformation? The work, the supervising the men required, the costs, would all fall to him. Was he up to it?

"Yes." Anything for Lily.

*I have faith in you* were Lutyen's last words to Rain. *Don't disappoint me*, Rain understood was his meaning.

Left alone and in charge of the grounds, Rain waivered under the crushing reality of what he'd proposed. He spent the next week walking the estate, meeting with the architect, watching his greenhouse renderings becoming larger and grander every time he made a suggestion to the man from York. In the evenings at his kitchen table as he pored over his drawings, he tried to calculate the number and kind of plants he would need, and fretted over designing a new garden around the pool in the courtyard every single day. It wasn't just the size of the greenhouse where he would need to store the vast amount of plants that was alarming, but more so the logistics involved in transforming the garden.

*How to get the plants from there to here?*

When the doubt became too much, he'd return to the ground staked for the greenhouse, often under the stars, and try to imagine the iron framework, the sheets of glass, the plants in pots crammed inside. The noise in moving such things. He'd need a small army, and how does a small army quickly and quietly transform a garden in a few hours?

Three times Rain cabled Lutyen. The plan, the scale, the cost! Surely the man had been too hasty in agreeing. The cables back: FORGET ABOUT THE MONEY. STOP. GET TO WORK. STOP. Meaning each day he knit his eyebrows and wailed like a schoolboy was a day less at labour.

The major was right and Rain, tormented by bouts of dry-heaving nausea when his nerves got the best of him, gave the order to start construction of the greenhouse. Trucks and heavy equipment rumbled in and out of the much-widened lane beyond the old barn. After a thin layer of rocky ground was scraped back and levelled, the foundation for the greenhouse was fitted with pipes for coal-fired steam heat, and the concrete poured. Although the structure would be out of sight from the main house, at times the noise was deafening. As November's numbing icy rain thickened into December snow, iron bones rose upon the foundations.

IN ONE OF HIS WEEKLY cables to Lutyen, Rain mentioned that tensions between miners at the nearby Nelson Pit and the mine's owners had grown steadily worse since the Armistice, boiling over now that Germany was using its coal in Europe as part of its reparations. Falling prices and the threat of longer workdays for English miners had sounded the call for a general strike. Without the heat from the coal, Rain said, the recently finished greenhouse would remain cold and empty.

Lutyen's response was a scathing editorial sent to various newspapers in London and the north, urging the government to crack down on belligerent miners. Get them back underground, he demanded. As one of the largest landowners in the region, he wrote, his need for a steady supply of cheap coal was not only important, but equally necessary to the financial health of the mines, if not the miners themselves.

ALL THROUGH THAT WINTER, trucks arrived at Walling carrying flowers and shrubs for the greenhouse: violet juliennes, Spanish carnations, hyacinths, irises, lilac bushes, jasmine and honey-suckles, tall yews, junipers, red-berry holly, bay spurge, laurel, anemones, narcissi, and jonquils.

Between working on the plans for a new garden for each day, tailored to each season, Rain scoured the countryside look-ing for trees. The farmers told Rain he was crazy, paying good money for a tree that would surely die after being pulled from the ground. But Rain had proved at Bon Sauveur that if you get enough of the root, you can move anything. He watched each transplant, overseeing as his men dug a square trench around the tree, then cut down to the bottom of the root ball, until Rain ordered the tree be sliced free. Wooden planks were boxed around its trunk and, once secured, the tree was hoisted onto the back of a truck. Some were replanted at Walling as part of Rain's grand design for the entire estate; others were left in their wooden containers to be easily moved back and forth from the greenhouse to the courtyard.

Every day a new detail demanded attention—an alteration to the greenhouse that could not wait, an ancient Scots pine outside of York so perfect that Rain just had to see. Often he worked late at his desk in the small cottage, waking in the morning with his fleshy cheek creased by the papers and books and pencils he'd slept on.

THE RINGING STARTLED RAIN; he hadn't expected it to be so loud. Lutyen had ordered the wire run to the cottage before he left, but this was the first time the telephone had worked. At the other end of the line was Evie, crackling and unhappy.

"What time is it?" he asked.

The woman hadn't been able to sleep and was in the kitchen warming a cup of milk. She had seen them through the window.

"Who?"

"Men with torches. I thought they were automobile lights."

"Why are you calling me?"

"At this hour? These men aren't coming to pay respects to my brother." Evie whispered heavily, as if the men on the road could hear. "I sent someone for the constable in the village and I have my brother's army pistol. If they try and get in here, I'll use it, but it looks like they're on the road, the new one to your greenhouse. You can't expect me to go out there and deal with them."

Rain pulled on his trousers, tucked his shirt underneath his canvas jacket. The chilly night air waited heavily outside his door. Low clouds and no moon. At this hour, who were these people? What did they want? Tall, wet grass left him soaked from the knees down as he hurried along the path to the greenhouse. Lily's greenhouse. Now he regretted not asking Evie to send down the few men who worked at the house, or at least rouse a battalion of maids armed with brooms and feather dusters.

Twenty, perhaps twenty-five men with faces that no amount of washing would make clean were pushing and shoving, swinging blazing torches, smelling of the bravado of drink and having trouble singing the right words about a Yorkshire girl who was champion and who didn't wear fancy under-clothes. They carried cloth bags slung about their shoulders and backs, and their fires reflected off the glass panes of the greenhouse.

"Whoa, there!" The man who called out wore a waistcoat and a scarf the colour of oxblood knotted about his neck. His long hair was tied back. He raised his arm. "You. Out o' the shadows where we can 'ave a look."

When Rain stepped into their light, the men laughed.

"How many others?"

"Just me."

The mob's leader swung open his arms and addressed his followers. "I told you *Lord* Lutyen had no stomach for a fight. See what he sends to defend 'is property."

Rain hoped it was dark enough to conceal how badly he trembled. "He's not here." His voice sounded higher when under stress, and that was funny to the men.

The group's leader strode easily over to Rain, close enough for Rain to smell the stink of whiskey and hard labour, to see a face not unfamiliar to a fist but still youthfully cocky, with a disarming grin that must have terrified the mothers of unmarried daughters in the village.

"We heard the master 'ere wasn't happy about his coal delivery, and bein' good lads one and all, we decided to bring it ourselves. In't that right, boys?"

Waving the torches, one and all agreed with their man.

A glass pane crumpled under a fist-sized clump of coal. Then another. The night air would make short lives of the delicate plants inside.

"Stop!"

Rain pushed his way to the greenhouse doors. More panes shattered. The piece of coal that clobbered Rain drew blood and he wobbled down to one knee.

"Out of the way, fool. I can't stop them and we've no row with you."

"Please, don't do this. The flowers, you'll destroy them."

"Your man Lutyen thinks to cut our wages, work us longer hours underground, and for what? Men like 'im need to be taught a lesson 'bout real work." The man gestured to the greenhouse. "So he's got fuckin' pansies when we don't even got a job. By Christ, I'll not tell you again. Get the hell out o' the way. Take 'er down, boys!"

Rain wiped the blood seeping into the corner of his mouth. "Wait, wait! Work? You want work? All of you. I can give you a job!"

"And who are you, making grand promises?"

"The gardener."

The man just had to laugh. "The fucking gardener, eh? Who gives you authority to hire us?"

"Andrew Lutyen. Look at this building. Go on, look at it."

"No! No! Take it down, Euan!" some in the crowd shouted.

But their leader waved for the others to fan out and follow him with their torches and for the first time, glimpsed the size of the glass walls.

"Mary, Mother o' the Lord, man," said Euan, "what's 'e doing here?"

"The plants in there are for a garden like nothing ever seen in England, and I can pay you all. Better wages than the mines."

"Why?"

"To save the greenhouse."

The others jeered, but Euan silenced them. "What's to stop that bastard from sending us down when 'e gets back?"

"There's too much work to be done. He'll need you. I give you my word."

"And he'll honour it?"

Rain knew the man didn't trust him, but so what? The feeling was mutual. And Lutyen? What would he say when he found out? Coal miners in his employ? Not thinking about that now. The greenhouse had to be saved. It'd be days before glaziers could replace the broken glass. Wood could take care of the few broken panes, but any more damage and Rain would lose everything.

He stuck out his hand and Euan shook it, but not before he spit on the ground and insisted he and the others would only work for Lutyen because they had hungry mouths to feed at home. "But know this," he concluded with a friendly pat on the shoulder, "fuck with me or my lads 'ere, and I'll see them gut you like a pig."

RAIN SET EUAN AND THE other coal miners to taking down the black-shingled blight on the far end of Walling's courtyard. The barn's Hanoverian timbers did not yield without a fight. When the oak beams, each the width of a man, were finally carried away, the view from the back of the great hall was clear through the courtyard down to the banks of the river.

Rain then removed the fountain Lutyen had had installed at the end of the pool: an enormous marble monstrosity of naked women cavorting with scarves and amphorae. Rain wanted to bury the cheap imitation, carved in Palermo, or perhaps have it ground into pebbles for the driveway. Instead he wrapped it in straw and crated it, in case Lutyen's bad taste demanded its return.

With the fountain gone, Rain constructed a narrow and shallow concrete trough that appeared to run from the end of the pool and cascaded over a series of gentle terraced slopes for over a hundred feet, drawing the eye down to the swift-moving river, wept over by willows, where discrete pumps returned the flow and allowed water to spout from various points when desired.

Next, he unearthed the Georgian folly, its stones accounted for, numbered, and rebuilt on a new foundation. The undergrowth from the nearby reflecting pool was dug out and the pool refilled. As part of the modernization, Rain fitted the round folly with windows and a wood stove along with cushioned benches.

None of these projects could have been completed without Euan and his men, but with a small army crawling over Walling came a small armies' concerns, mostly in the form of petty rivalries, illnesses, and foibles. Thank God for Euan. For while the man's work consisted mostly of lording over his men, a cigarette clinging to his lips, and smelling of the drink by midday, Rain could confidently determine the what and leave the how to his lieutenant.

With Walling slowly tamed, its ancient retaining walls and buttresses along walking paths repaired or replaced, and pipes strung underground to keep the fountains and pools fresh, Rain struggled with his biggest problem. His plan for Lily's garden depended on how he'd get hundreds of bedding plants and mature trees from the greenhouse to the courtyard and back, each night. So many men on the grounds would be impossible to co-ordinate, and their booted feet would crush delicate plants and turf.

"You need your own train," said Euan as he followed Rain through the densely packed and humid greenhouse.

"Yes, with a railroad and stationmaster."

"I ain't joking, mate. Narrow gauge, small engine, like we use in the mines. Set the tracks a few feet down in the ground and run 'em behind that hill. No one'd see a thing." At Rain's bemused expression, Euan grabbed the pencil from his hand and began to sketch. "A factory I know in Newcastle'd build it."

They would need a special railcar to transport the plants, one fitted with a crane that could be unfolded to lift large containers and trees into position inside the courtyard. And all this could be done silently, Euan added. So long as the wheels of the railcars were sheathed in heavy rubber, along with the tops of the tracks.

RAIN CHOSE SEVERAL POLLARDED ORANGE trees, their root systems secure in wooden crates, to test the new railcar and crane system. He watched the miners load them onto the miniature train, its tracks extending inside the vast greenhouse. The trees would test the crane's load-bearing abilities.

Rain fretted. "Gently. Careful!"

The crane lifted an orange tree, then slowly lowered it onto the flatbed railcar. Shortly, the train edged out of the greenhouse on its sunken tracks.

Rain pulled off his hat and wiped his chin with the back of his hand.

At the courtyard, Euan gave the order to lift the tree over the low wall built to conceal the garden's mechanics. The crane unfurled, and again the tree rose, but as it was about to swing over the wall and into the garden, the offside weight slowly pulled the railcar from the track.

"Drop it! Drop it or we'll lose the whole train!" Euan called out.

"No, I can save it."

Rain darted underneath the swinging orange tree and tried to right the weight enough that the tree could be spared, but he fell when the night air snapped with shot. Bullets bounced and sparked off the train, dug angrily into the ground.

The round ball of orange tree swung back and forth on its loud-creaking chain, and the men crouched and ducked, shouts and gunfire resounding through the grounds. When the chain snapped, the tree fell, breaking its trunk in half. Then Rain crawled towards Euan and tried to staunch the bleeding.

"YOU COULD HAVE BEEN KILLED."

"And miss seeing the gov' cry over a tree?"

Rain was surprised by how intensely a flash of hatred came for this man, even as Euan lay on his sofa, the blood seeping into the horsehair and dripping onto the floor.

"Will I live?"

Flesh wound to the thigh. Messy. Torn trouser leg now the colour of his knotted scarf, but yes, Euan would live to make jest of another day.

Rain filled a glass with Lily's whiskey. "Who were they?" he asked.

"How in th' hell would I know?"

"Because you had a lot say when we carried you back here, but not once did you wonder who fired."

"Ah, just the pain talkin'."

"I think you know."

Euan emptied the glass. "If I did know, not that I do, but I'd say the general strike's not making things easy at the pits. Maybe some boys don't like that our women got money for the shops."

"How are we to work if we get shot at?"

"Men got families. They're hungry."

If Rain could see to putting something their way, Euan figured they'd find some other place for shooting practice. But, there was the matter of what his lordship'd say.

"You give me your word they'll leave us be?" Rain asked, guessing from Euan's schoolboy smile that the attack was nothing more than a ruse.

"For food? I can say that."

WHEN LILY AND ANDREW RETURNED from abroad, Evie telephoned the cottage to tell Rain that her brother and that woman, tired after the ride from London, had retired after a light supper. Lily, however, wanted it mentioned that she especially liked the sweet william and the fiery azaleas by the pool, although Mr. Lutyen said there'd be words over the missing nymphs.

Rain sat alone at his table for a few minutes, numb, although it was not cold. After all the practice, the moment had finally arrived. No mistakes, no delays, and most importantly, no sound.

At midnight, he joined Euan at the greenhouse where creamy white viburnum clusters and budding rhododendrons shoved yellow daffodil bells up against the panes. His men shuffled expectantly under plumes of tobacco smoke, silent and excited. Moths fluttered foolishly near to the torches under a clear sky. The heavens would not always be so generous or the Yorkshire wind so absent when the garden changed, but tonight, Rain gave thanks. As soon as the last of the lights in the house went dark,

Euan saw to the quick loading of the railcars inside the greenhouse, hobbling but still effective on his crutch. Men carried the smaller plants and shrubs up by hand, while the others attached chains dangling from iron beams from the glass ceiling to trees and pallets of flowers, lifting and swinging them onto the flatbed cars quickly and with only a whisper.

Crickets chirped over the quiet *putt-putt-putt* of the gas engine as the train made the short ride to the courtyard, the men clinging to the sides of the railcars. When it arrived, they jumped off, raised the hoist, and strung cables to the corners of the wooden boxes overflowing with orange and red azaleas that were sunk level with the paving surrounding the pool. With Rain's hand signal, box by box, the colourful blooms that had greeted Lily and Lutyen on their return home were plucked from the beds beside the pool's paving stones and replaced with similar-sized wooden crates painted with *trompe l'oeil* to resemble stone. Each one contained a full-size flowering orange tree. With a quick sweep of the disturbed soil from the switch, the oranges looked as if they had scented the air over the water since the days of Elizabeth.

While some of the men lowered the trees into place, others rolled up the lengths of turf that lay along the outer walls of the house, replacing them with long inlaid wooden boxes crowded with white, yellow, red, and purple tulips. Then they set out lilies in clay pots where the sweet william had adorned the terraced lawn, and the transformation was almost complete. Two unwieldy flats of ornately configured boxwood, set into place over the terrace just below Lily's balcony, turned the stone paving into a leafy, painstakingly clipped geometric parterre, and the garden's first transformation was complete.

The hoist lifted away the returning plants, and the men jumped onto the sides of the train in retreat. An hour before dawn, all were sweating behind the humid glass walls of the greenhouse.

Rain could not see Euan making his way home on his wounded leg, so he offered him his unused bed.

Sitting at his kitchen table, Rain waited. What would Lily think? Would the garden make her happy? What about Lutyen? All those invoices. Maybe it was too much. And what about the man snoring upstairs? He and the others, their wages, would take some explaining. Yes, he'd been manipulated, but Rain couldn't think about that now. The garden needed a plan for the next transformation. Explanations had to be carefully crafted. The other projects about the estate wanted attention. All in good time. He would take a few minutes, just to close his eyes....

SHE APPEARED LIKE A DREAM. Her wrap was light and dotted with wet and the fur trim of the collar was matted. Spring in New York must be kinder. The cloth bell on her head was upturned and pulled down low, securing twin curls on each side. Lily's hands grabbed at the heat from the stove as the late morning storm broke hard against the kitchen window. When he awoke, his back was stiff, his chair creaked, and yet these annoyances did not dispel the dream of her.

"How uncomfortable you look there, my darling thing."

Lily pulled off her hat and tossed it on the table. From her pocket came a small brown box tied with white ribbon.

"When I woke up this morning and saw what you did, for me, I just had to come and thank you. I hope you like it."

Rain took the box in his hands, wished the moment never had to be opened, ruined, left to fade. Inside he found a scarf, blue and green and sturdy.

"You really should have something around your neck when you work outside and Andrew said something from Barney's would do. We can't have you catching a cold, like I will, no doubt, after today. Look at me. I've already forgotten about spring in Manhattan. I'm ruined."

She was just as beautiful as ever, always.

"Too early for a real drink? Tea then. You have no idea how much I've missed you. You do have tea? Did I tell you that Andrew is on the warpath?"

Rain pointed to the tin of Yorkshire Gold on the shelf. Lily. Making tea for him.

"He didn't like the garden?"

"Oh, he loved it. Surprised as I was. No, I think *shocked* is the better word. He does love that I love it, but such a great deal of money. The bills, and Evie can't stop talking about all those men you hired."

"He's that angry?"

She tapped out several teaspoons of loose tea. "Ignore it. Andrew's been scowling for weeks now. Something about the markets. We hardly enjoyed ourselves in America at all." Suddenly angry, Lilly pulled open the cupboard looking for cups and almost banged Rain in the face. "But really? Men from the coal pits here at Walling? Andrew says they're communists. He'd shoot them but apparently Evie's misplaced his pistol. What were you thinking?"

"That 'e mustn't disappoint such a beautiful lady," said Euan from the doorway, standing with his cane and impish grin, buttoning his vest over his open shirt.

"Oh."

He bowed, but overly so.

"Lily, this is one of the communists from the coal pits."

Tea was forgotten.

"You've been injured."

"A bullet happily taken in your service, ma'am."

Too young to be a ma'am, but she seemed too charmed to rebuke him.

"You must let me take a look at that bandage." Lily glanced at Rain. "Miracles in the garden you may do, but a doctor you are not. Why was one not called?"

Lily tugged off her wrap and hung it over the back of a chair. Could Rain boil water and find something clean to use as a bandage? Euan was to go back to the sofa and pull up the leg of his trouser.

Rain ran his fingers over the blue and green. Too nice to wear, and soft. In the other room Euan spoke and Lily laughed and the water took so very long to boil.

RAIN DISCOVERED THE PAGODA in the autumn while men thinned a stand of alders by the river. Thanks to its pitched foundation, the tall narrow structure leaned with age against a truculent beech. Gone were many of the slate tiles on the five-tiered roof. Inside the base was room for a bench for two, though presently it provided storage for a birchbark canoe. The canoe intrigued Euan, who after carrying it out was sure he could patch it and make it usable. Lutyen thought the pagoda, with its cracked and warped panels of red lacquer and traces of gold detail, worth restoring and told Rain to make it happen.

"Lily loves what you did with that place by the pond. Let this be my Christmas gift to her."

Yes, Lily did like the folly. She took a book out there every afternoon, precisely at two, though she never seemed to open it. One afternoon Rain saw her there with Euan. Just talking, sitting on the steps, nothing more really. So why was his chest thumping like he'd witnessed a murder? He had hurried away before he saw something that would need to be confessed.

If only Euan would go back to the coal pits, underground, away from Walling, away from Lily, gone with the rest of the men who'd mostly returned with the end of the general strike. *Good riddance*, said Lutyen, who'd taken a fair amount of convincing from Rain to keep them in the first place; he and his sister generally didn't agree upon much, but they both seemed convinced they'd end up shot in a pit like the Romanovs with so many Reds about.

But Euan didn't care to go back underground, not with so many delights above, as he put it. A good worker, he helped expand the greenhouse and oversaw the laying of more tracks for the train. *Let me work on the pagoda*, he had said, and spent long days at the site by the river, racing against winter to finish it. In the evenings he refurbished the canoe, a Canadian relic, he believed. And still he found time to sit with Lily by the pond.

Lutyen was happy that Lily voluntarily spent more time at home, complaining less about missing everything in London, even if it required more parties, more guests, more opportunities for the smart set to see the changing gardens at Walling—the most sought-after invitation of any season. But Rain was not happy. And he knew very well that Lily did not need another place like the folly, away from prying eyes and wagging tongues. So Rain blamed it on lightning when he told Lutyen that the pagoda had unexpectedly burnt to the ground.

RAIN SLID THE CANOE ONTO the water and jumped in. It sank low. Euan had done a good job patching the birch rind. The cedar ribs creaked; the still water ruptured; teardrops fell from the finely carved oar. At the bend, the current turned in on itself and Rain stopped paddling, slowly drifting in circles with day peaking over the eastern hills above him. Foolish, he knew, but he imagined being here with Lily, her fingers trailing in the water as they cut through the mist under white willows dripping silvery green crowns, while early-rising lapwings helped carry dawn over the estate.

From here he created hundreds of measured drawings. Old glories to be preserved: brown and yellow rudbeckia and columbine and clusters of bird's-eye primrose. Weeds to banish: ragwort, curly dock, and creeping thistle. Boundaries to be softened. View lines to be blurred, vistas opened. Did he go for the vagaries of fashion or demand a style that would please not only now but a generation from now? Some plants last only a handful of weeks, while trees took decades to mature. The diversity of fields, forest, pasture, riverbanks, swamp, heather-covered hillocks, the ever-changing sky above them all...a wind that eroded and felled. Winter with its ice and silence. How was he to bring cohesion to the wholes within the whole, while allowing each part to thrive? To complement? And if Rain did manage the miraculous, what guarantee could he have that time and neglect would not undo it all in just a handful of seasons.

DRESSED IN KHAKIS, A LEATHER satchel slung over his shoulder, the photographer, Rain thought, would look more at ease taking pictures of elephants in Rhodesia. Not much of a talker, it fell to the young *Town & Country* editor, who ignored Rain, to assure Lily effusively, and with jazzy gestures, that the camera guy was the real McCoy. *Covered the war, then Hollywood. Pretty much the same thing.* The New York magazine editor laughed at his own wit. He assured them the photographer would do a swell job on the Walling spread.

Rain explained during a tour of the humid greenhouse that there were over 700 plants, 175 varieties.

"Why so many, Mrs. Lutyen?"

"The climate here is harsh," said Rain because Lily had no idea. "Some plants, when we change the garden, barely survive a day outside."

"Is this the darling miniature train I've heard about?"

The photographer snapped a picture as Euan explained its manufacture in Newcastle.

"Designed and built just for this garden?"

"Every detail," said Lutyen.

The tour moved under the palms. Lily fidgeted with the long strand of pearls about her neck.

"Is it true the Prince of Wales asked to see your garden?"

"My wife and I would be delighted to host His Royal Highness."

"So would your sister, Andrew. You know she would."

"So tell me, Mrs. Lutyen, just how does it all work?"

"I don't know the first thing about it, really. We make everyone come inside and close the drapes. When we reopen them, the garden is changed. You'll have to ask the gardener here how he does it."

"I see. It must cost a great deal of money, Mr. Lutyen?"

"You Americans always want to know the cost."

"Priceless," said the photographer, unexpectedly. "Can't you see this is a labour of love?"

Everyone looked at Rain.

"I can assure you," said Lutyen, "our gardener is paid quite handsomely."

WHEN THE EIGHT-PAGE ARTICLE appeared in *Town & Country* in the spring of 1929, Lily told Rain that he mustn't be offended that his picture wasn't included. She knew the gardens were because of him. The magazine catered to wealthy American matrons and debutants, so naturally the publisher would want that picture of Euan instead. *He did photograph well, didn't Rain think so?* Besides, wasn't it enough that with Walling's garden famous in the United States, an invitation to the Prince would now be favourably received?

NEWLY MONOGRAMED TABLE LINEN, THE rims of crystal glasses, the temperature of the wine, everything reviewed, checked, then re-examined by Evie. Even the weather, after June days of unsea-sonably sleet-filled winds and low blue clouds railing against the tops of the surrounding hills, had cleared and warmed. The first of the automobiles from London arrived before noon. Rain and his crew had been trimming the lawns for several days. He now fretted that his choice of design for the courtyard garden was too simple, but there was no time to change the plans now. Lily said not to worry, she was sure that whatever he chose would delight everyone. She almost sounded like the old Lily when she said that, free of pretense and enthusiasm for Americanisms. Her husband and sister-in-law may have been ready to kneel under the impending Royal visit, but Lily was too busy trying on new frocks.

From the shelter of the alders outside her window, Rain watched and wondered what she'd wear to meet the Prince. He knew she liked silver, and wore it well. Yellow too. But burgundy, now that was the colour that best lit up her eyes.

Lily shook her short hair free of water as the towel fell. Her breasts were small and white and quite pointed. Some thought amused her, as she stood there naked in front of a window overlooking a patch of wild wood, in no hurry to cover herself.

Rain had found this shaded place quite by chance, hidden, with a direct view into her room. He left it untouched amongst all of his changes to the landscape. Leaning against the bark, he felt himself harden. He gripped himself roughly and bit the bottom of his lip to suck back a groan. Closing his eyes, he pulled his cock from his trousers, stroking, imagined her breasts in his hands, a soft, trailing kiss. Left gently, and wetly on a perfect face. Then he sprayed his semen on the veined buckthorn leaves before him.

*Lily.*

He caught his pounding breath.

She was gone from the window.

Rain pushed himself off the tree and buttoned his trousers. He had to get to the greenhouse and see to the loading of the train. The lights had been turned on over the pool and flickered through the dark canopy of leaves along with the nearby glow from Euan's cigarette.

WHEN THE GUESTS WERE LED from the great hall and into the courtyard, they broke into Hurray! Huzzah! Bravo! at the splendor of the garden: urns of shiny copper beech with rounded crowns alternating with balls of boxwood flanked the pool, surrounded by a sea of heaving yarrow crowned with flat-topped clusters of red blossoms from which holly bushes, clipped into dolphins, appeared to jump. The jazz band gave its best "God Save the King."

Rain had done it all without Euan.

The man hadn't taken his post by the greenhouse train, hadn't helped to position the trees, hadn't seen Rain angrily snap one of the young beeches with his bare hands because of his impending humiliation. Euan had done nothing, except surely run to Lily to tell her the gardener had been paddling himself like a schoolboy

outside her window while his hands, his coarse filthy hands fit
for nothing but a seam of coal, caressed her skin, touched *his*
Lily in places Rain dared not name. He imagined shoving that
broken length of beech into Euan's face, anything to silence the
laugher. *Her* laughter. At him, her darling thing. And what about
the major? What hell would there be to pay when he found out?

Rain, burning from the shame, fled the horrid applause.


HE WAS DRUNK, HORRIBLY DRUNK, but not so drunk as to miss
hearing the cries that came suddenly from the river. Rain pushed
away the bottle and pulled himself up from the chair. The room
spun about him dizzily. Opening his door, he heard the watery
thrashing, grabbed hold of the kerosene light on the porch, then
pushed unsteadily through the ragusa densely lining the path. A
dull fog clung weakly to the reeds at the river's edge. Another
hollow cry rattled against the otherwise calm night. Seeing the
light, a woman screamed through a mouth full of water.

Lily!

Rain tugged off his boots and waded in, mercifully sobered
by the icy jolt as he dove and swam. The last of the mist pulled
away in front of him as he reached the overturned canoe to which
Euan frantically clung.

"I can't swim!" he called out, as it got caught up in the current at the bend.

But where was Lily?

There—going under, only an arm's length away.


RAIN PLACED LILY GENTLY ON the sofa, shivering, and tucked all
the blankets he could find around her, then made a fire.

When he put the mug into her hands, Lily shook her head.

"Whiskey. Drink," he said.

Rain glanced back to the door, to the river, the fast-moving water.

Lily wiped her eyes with the corner of the blanket. She emptied the mug. "I've got to get back to the house. Andrew will be worried."

Rain gently forced her back against the sofa. "He can't know you were out there."

She inhaled as if her reply required a store of breath, then she looked away from the truth.

"Stay here until your clothes are dry. Fix your hair. Tell your husband you came to thank me. When they find him—"

Lily's hand covered a weak cry.

"When they find him, they must believe he was out there on his own."

She nodded.

He refilled their mugs. Rain, drinking more than he should, felt the long, exhausting day threaten to pull him under, only to be pulled back by her gaze, shining and questioning, upon him.

"What is it?"

"Nothing," she said. "Have another. I know you love me, don't you?"

THE GREY DAWN IN THE casement window was unfamiliar because the room was unfamiliar. The bed unfamiliar. The memory of her kisses, the smell of her on the sheets, on his hands, unfamiliar. Rain was upstairs.

He pulled off his blankets and sat up. Naked. No fire. The cottage was cold and damp. His head throbbed as he ran his hands across his face, remembered thrashing in the water, then hastily rolled over and retched on the floor.

As he wiped his mouth with the back of his hand, he saw her wrap, still damp from the river, tossed carelessly as a lie over the end of the bed.

*Ficus benjamina*

# 1933

The two elderly women huddling under the umbrella juggled their guidebook and pointed to the once-gilded Apollo riding the waves. To Rain, sitting on the bench nearby, tightening the scarf about his neck, Apollo looked more like a weary farmer plowing stagnant green muck. Such was the atmosphere at Versailles that damp winter day, which had kept most visitors away and the groundskeepers huddling for warmth over fires stoked in drums under the windows of Marie Antoinette's boudoir. More than the disappointing sleet was that Versailles, once the playground of the Sun King, was now a tourist attraction of stinking, ill-kept fountains clogged with dead cats, amateurishly replanted flowerbeds, and peeling palace walls surrendering to the invasion of pigweed.

"You understand that I can't keep her any longer," Lutyen said about Walling when he had to let Rain go.

Lord knows, the man had tried everything in those years after the markets crashed, even resorting to what amounted to deals with the devil that, Rain saw, kept the man awake, bottle in hand. But the night Rain pulled Lily from the river was the last time the gardens of Walling had changed. The Prince had not even appeared that evening, bedridden in London with a head cold. Nor had Euan shown his face, though that was only to be expected from those bloody Yorkshire miners, Lutyen had reasoned. Disappeared just when you had come to depend on them.

Rain was sure the man's body would wash into some farmer's field or snag a fisherman's line, but the truth of what happened that night seemed destined for the sea.

Lily was gone when Rain next came around to the house with his accounts. To Paris, Lutyen said, sounding like a man not yet cooled from the heat of an argument, but who blamed himself. *Not to worry. When she comes back, all will be forgiven.* Walling would return to full glory.

Both men told themselves that for a long time.

But Lily did not come back from Paris, and one by one, the household staff was let go.

"It's no good. I have to cut my losses, my friend," Lutyen confessed to Rain one evening, smoking by the pool, now thick with leaves under a benign evening. His sister had returned unhappily to London, blaming her brother for the loss of the family fortune, and quite sure she'd never manage on the tiny annuity he provided. Rain was the last to go. Until that day he worked the grounds as best as he could, determined that Lily's home must always be ready and as she left it, even if he could no longer be blind to the falling glass in the empty greenhouse, and the train rusting quietly on its tracks.

To SAVE THE FARE, Rain walked the twenty kilometres back to Montmartre. By the Trocadéro one of his boots took on water. There'd be no money for a repair. Not a single job had come his way since he'd arrived in Paris. Those friends and acquaintances of Lutyen's he could remember from visits to Walling were now the Depression's walking dead. *I'd love to hire you, my good man*, he had heard on the doorstep of a now shabby townhouse, *but you know how it is.* What money Lutyen had paid Rain over his years of service appeared to have been buried under the collapse of his English bank. Enough money, his wet foot reminded him, to live dryly. He began each day at the Paris branch, inquiring if any funds could be salvaged.

*No monsieur, try again tomorrow.*

On the rue de Monceau, Rain passed a patisserie, its window crowded with fresh loaves of bread. Inside, at the counter, a young woman and her child clapped their hands as the owner sprinkled icing sugar over a tray of *petits fours*, and then, with silver tongs, placed them carefully into a cardboard box. Wearing a double-breasted navy coat, the little girl twisted and kicked her legs excitedly.

Strange as it was, the gesture reminded him of Lily. Something about her childish fidgeting, her smile looking for a place to land, or perhaps only his longing to have a baby with Lily, since that day he first saw her laughing in the mud.

Not that Rain had followed her to Paris, he reminded himself. But he imagined he saw her often—in a curl peeking out from a bonnet, a half-moon crease at the side of a mouth, a similarly quick and purposeful walk—and each time it stopped him just long enough to realize it wasn't her.

Then in the glass, Rain caught his reflection.

Pulling his fraying coat tight about his neck, he turned away hungrily from the sweet scent of rising bread, clutching the few francs he had left in his pocket.

RAIN COULD NOT STAND UPRIGHT in the room he let under the eaves. When the weather blew in, a chipped jug on the floor by the sofa that was also his bed caught the drips, while the roof tiles rattled with the gurgling rush of the downpour outside as it bounced into the street below. He had a hotplate for when he had something to eat, and there was a toilet down two flights of narrow, uneven stairs.

The owner of the building had not leased the attic space before, but like many of Paris's once well-heeled, monsieur was reduced to renting out every available inch if he was to keep up appearances. The tenant on the ground floor was a man with a large black dog, the kind which looked to Rain like a small bear. He thought the man was a writer, for often he'd see him sitting in the bistro across the street, the dog guarding his feet and growling if anyone got too close, while the man jotted furiously in a notebook. Perhaps he was a novelist who one day would be famous. Then Rain would buy his book, remembering how hungry and threadbare the author, and himself, once were.

Rain had not met the second-floor tenant until that evening as he returned from his day at Versailles, although he often fell asleep to the music from her gramophone. The woman wore an orange turban and tried to keep a loud floral dressing gown from falling open as, with her free hand, she dragged a gangly tree in a glazed Chinese pot across the landing, puffing frustratedly all the while on a cigarette.

"Whatcha looking at, honey?"

Black skin and red hair.

"You the fella that lives in the attic? Thought so. Hear you stomping around up there." She let go of the pot and stood. "Call me Bricky, honey. Yeah, nice to know you, too. Say, you look like you could lend me a hand."

A trail of leaves led back into the woman's flat.

"That's why it's going out. Wouldn't you know it, I'm staying here while my friend's doing this little cabaret act in Berlin and I've done killed her favourite. You think she'll know it's gone when she gets back?"

A leaf fell at Rain's touch. "Did you move it recently?"

"Had to. Couldn't see out the window."

"Ficus. They don't like being moved. Or draughts."

"You know something about plants?"

"A little."

"You think you can save it?"

Rain looked the plant over closely.

"My friend Mabel's a doll, but she's a bitch with a temper. I'd really hate to say I killed her tree, you know what I mean? Why couldn't she have a cat? All the strays around here, I could replace that without her catching on."

Rain carried the plant back into the woman's flat and placed it behind the sofa by the window. He checked the dryness of the soil. Filling two bowls with water, he placed them on top of the nearby radiators.

"Ficus like it humid," he said.

RAIN WOKE EARLY TO THE unfamiliar sound of knocking on his door. The woman from downstairs stood waiting behind it, with ostrich feathers in her hair—one broken—and a deep-cut, floor-length black dress that clung to her wide hips and thick middle. She smelled of stale tobacco and gin and clearly had no intention of apologizing for the hour.

"Honey, you've saved my hide," she said, holding onto the door-frame. "Did like you said, and not a single leaf down for a week."

The patient was on the mend—now she needed him to do his doctoring on the palms in her bar on the rue Pigalle. Bricky handed Rain her card.

"This evening. Don't be late. I'll make it worth your while."

"Are you sure Miss...Missus—"

"Just Bricky, honey."

"I mean—"

"Oh that? Your face? Oh, sweet baby, yeah, you're ugly, but drunks only swing at the pretty boys. Everyone's going to be too afraid of that patchwork of yours to misbehave."

Rain didn't know what to think about Bricky. He'd certainly never met anyone like her. She brought the tail end of a party with her, even when she was alone. But he wasn't giving up the only prospect of a job since he'd arrived in France just because it meant working for a woman. A coloured woman. Who had her own business. Come nightfall, he was standing outside the woman's bar on the rue Pigalle. BRICKTOP'S, right there, over the door.

Leather curtains, guarded by a towering Argentinian with arms folded against an impressive chest, kept out prying eyes. He tried brushing Rain away with a broken mishmash of languages, saying that if he needed a handout, a church nearby had soup going in the cellar. If he was surprised to see the card Rain offered him, he didn't let on. He stuck his head behind the curtains, shouted for someone named Albert, and something about *madame*. Several minutes later, Rain was escorted past red and black banquettes dimly lit with lamps and adorned with fresh ashtrays, though the air stank of day-old pomade, sweaty wool, and Chanel No. 5.

The musicians on the dais were tuning. Drapes and languid oversized palms lined the walls. Bricky sat at the end of the long bar, behind which three waiters with trim waists mindlessly polished glasses with white cloths. A pile of bills was on her left, and a box full of francs and notes lay on her right. Next to her sat a girl blacker than Bricky, maybe fifteen, drinking a bottle of Coca-Cola through a straw. She was dressed in what looked to Rain like a school uniform, and she sulkily turned her face away when she caught him staring.

Bricky hopped off her stool. "Overalls? In a nightclub? Go cut me a switch, honey."

"I'm a gardener."

"Bonnie Prince Eddie comes in here to have a good time and you looking like you took a wrong turn at the relief line. It'll put him off spending what I charge for champagne if he starts thinking about the poor."

"The Prince of Wales comes here?"

"Honey, everyone in Paris comes through these doors eventually." She scribbled an address on a piece of paper. "Monsieur Lepin over on the rue d'Orchampt is the best tailor in Paris, and he owes me a favour. Well? Why are you standing there?"

"Rather late to be visiting a tailor?"

Bricky waved Rain away. "Tell him you're working for me. He'll know what I want."

BRICKY COULDN'T PAY RAIN; like she said, wasn't she hard pressed to pay herself from that big pile of francs at the end of each night? He was, after all, just watering a palm here, a leafy thing there, but he could eat as much as he wanted, seeing as how she was on her milk and banana diet, so long as he kept his hands off the champagne and liquor; that was for paying guests only. Bricky wasn't running no flim-flam joint and if he cheated her or one of her customers, he'd find himself ass-first on the curb. But the beer was free, and Rain could help himself to the cigarettes.

Everyone smoked at Bricktop's. They made it look so glamorous and easy, cigarettes floating on fingertips. Rain still smoked like a soldier huddled in a trench, but he found that if he smoked Gitanes all day he wasn't so hungry before he could get to the club and fill up with one of its famous roast beef sandwiches. He just had to watch for pigeons when hanging his tuxedo from his window to air out the stale tobacco smell.

Bricktop's towering palms and elephant ears in hammered copper urns required minimal attention and each table only got a handful of fresh flowers. No need to go overboard in a room lit for the diamonds to sparkle, as Bricky said. *Besides, no one looks at the daisies.* Dressed like one of the well-heeled, a pair of pruning scissors in his pocket, Rain could go about his business, sometimes humming along to Bricky's English friend, Mabel Mercer, singing "Love for Sale" by the piano, sometimes wondering who was that getting ferociously drunk at Cole Porter's reserved table by the bar, all the while ignored by everyone, except maybe the teenage girl whose eyes followed him around the room. At first, he thought it was his face. She'd sit at the bar until the club opened, then disappear under a sullen cloud into the back office. Bricky called her Edmée.

"But you ignore that girl, honey. She belongs to a friend."

The thin, blond man in shabby gabardine at a nearby table tapped his glass with a spoon.

"Song! Song!"

He climbed on his chair. "I'll not stop tapping my glass," he said, and the others simply must join him, until Bricky gave a song.

"Is he crazy?"

"Scotty's just drunk. Ask me, his wife Zelda's the crazy one."

Bricky took to the dais. "All right, suckers! You'll know this one from my good pal, Cole."

The woman wasn't much of a singer, and her gyrations reminded Rain of how a skeleton might move, but the frantic saxophone, the clarinet, and her woeful tale of Miss Otis shooting her lover and getting lynched by the mob, and therefore unable to do lunch, soon had the dance floor crowded before her.

Bowing to enthusiastic applause, she pulled up her skirts and gave her hand to Rain to help her off the stage.

"Hold it right there, sonny," she said, clutching at the collar of a handsome well-formed youth. "You think I didn't see you? Mohammad Reza, I told you, you're too young to be at my gaming tables. Why aren't you at that fancy school in Switzerland? Are you here by yourself?"

"I don't need a babysitter, Bricky, and what do I want school for? It's more fun here."

"Miss Bricky to you, young man. And you need school because one day you'll be a king, or whatever it is Persia has. Do you well to learn a thing or two about the value of your people's money, not just how to lose it. Now, you know what the Shah made me promise."

The youth looked like he was about to launch a defense.

"Don't. He's your father and he pays your tab." Bricky took him by the arm and led him to the curtained entrance. "Be a sweetheart and go home, and consider yourself lucky I won't tell anyone about tonight." She tapped him on the face and smiled.

Watching Bricky work her way back into the crowd, the young man reached for a cigarette.

"Light?"

Rain reached into his pocket.

"You work here, don't you?" the youth asked.

"I'm a gardener."

"Not much of a job."

Eyes too young to be bored surveyed the crowd of gowns and tuxes with the thin, indulgent smile of the rich and spoiled that Rain often saw here.

"Shall I call you cab?"

The doorman could see to that. There was a hierarchy, after all.

The young fellow reached into his pocket. "But I seem to have misplaced my last note."

He might have been born in a tuxedo, but he still had the look of a boy about him. And at that moment, one with no way home.

Rain handed over his last five francs. "For the taxi."

The young man grinned, flicked his cigarette into the potted palm, and tapped Rain on the elbow. "Thanks, old man."

BRICKY SAW TO IT THAT anyone who still had money must have Rain do their garden, or the ratty bits of nature in behind their townhouse, or even the urns on their terrace. She was good like that. He got paid, too, and soon moved out of his room and into a furnished flat across the hall from Bricky, where he could stand upright and didn't have to descend several flights of stairs to pee. Working elsewhere also made Rain feel less beholden to Bricktop's, where he kept the palms lush and the elephant ears flapping, then enjoyed a quiet beer at the bar before Bricky began the evening with "Halloo, suckers!"

Edmée sat beside him. "Light?" she asked, sounding somewhere between Dutch and English.

He offered her one.

The girl leaned in, lit her cigarette, then tossed the smoke down her throat very much like a woman. Her transformation was amazing.

"I found this dress in her closet. Fits me better, don't you think?"

"Does Bricky know?"

Edmée exhaled. "She only wants that I sit in her room all night reading stupid schoolbooks, nobody talking to me. How do I go to London if I don't practice my English? But you help me. How about I do something for you, no charge?"

Rain stubbed his cigarette in the tray.

"No? But maybe you wait for someone? You sit here every night; you watch that door. A woman? A special woman?"

The girl was smart, and Bricky was wrong. Not everyone in Paris came through the door.

"Maybe it's not a woman?" Edmée rolled one of her naked shoulders as if to say this schoolgirl was beyond the revulsion of such perversions.

"Is that my dress?"

Most times Bricky worked the image of slightly tipsy party girl, hard. Watching her tally receipts every night, eyes focused, fingers running down lists of numbers, Rain knew better than to come between her and her francs. But Rain had never expected this. Raging bulldog mad and, maybe, even scared.

"You get out back and take it off. And scrub that greasepaint off your face, too."


THE LAST FEW PATRONS SLUMPED drunkenly over their tabletops and the rue Pigalle was a pale canyon in the pre-dawn when Rain finished transplanting one of the palms that had grown too big for its urn. He'd waited until now so he could remove his bowtie and jacket.

"Drink, honey?" The hot round tip of her cigarette glowed in backlit dark. Friend of Bricky's, some hotshot society photographer did up the theatrical lights for her so that even Rain looked, if not good, at least not bad. In front of her, an open, half-empty bottle. "Sit."

He did, and Bricky filled a glass.

"Long day?" he asked.

"Always is. That's how I like 'em."

They touched their glasses together and drank.

"You know, when I first opened my place, you could have a drink with a future king, maybe dance with a Russian countess in diamonds she'd hidden from the Bolsheviks up her breadbox, never guessing they were paste and that she'd pawned the real things for rent. Good times, honey, good times. Now it's all these movie people from America. Directors, producers, starlets parading about in tight dresses, just to show off their tits. Don't get me wrong, I'm American too, but new money ain't got a thimbleful of class, not between the whole fucking lot of 'em."

However, they did keep large Paris homes with even larger gardens, and their obsession with novelty kept Rain designing lounge areas around pools and pastoral views from upstairs galleries.

"You know why they come here?"

"You make them feel at home." Rain wished gin wasn't the booze on offer, but he drank all the same.

"And you wouldn't want to see anything happen to my home, would you?" Bricky wasn't sounding so dreamy. She was leaning back against the upholstered booth, one hand thrown wearily over the top of her head, staring at him. *Pay attention*, the look on her face said. "You hear of a man named Olly Lardet?"

No, Rain hadn't.

"Boxer. Bit of a career in the ring. Figured out a way he could make more money without getting beaten up every night."

"Doing what?"

"Luxury goods. Import. The kind you can't buy in shops. For people with discerning tastes." Bricky topped up Rain's gin. "You know that fire at the bar on rue Turgot? The broken windows on Turdaine?"

Sure. It's all those finch-like bartenders of hers chirped about. Gangsters.

"It's what happens when you don't buy protection from Lardet." The hand holding her cigarette rested on the edge of the table.

"Is that legal?"

Bricky was too weary to laugh.

"What about the *gendarmes*?"

"Yes, dear boy, what about them?"

"So, you pay."

"Of course not. I'm from Chicago. I work too damn hard for every franc just to give it away to a thug. I got a deal with Lardet; he leaves Bricktop's alone." Ashes, delicately tapped into the tray. "Edmée. She's very beautiful, isn't she?"

"I guess so."

"Lardet brought her from the Ivory Coast."

"His daughter?"

"His property. I keep an eye on her when he's away, or when he's busy."

"She's a kid, Bricky."

"Don't let the uniform fool you. Like I said. I made a deal, and Lardet doesn't like anyone chatting up what's his."

Rain pushed his glass away and got up, but Bricky wasn't done.

"People see things. They don't understand. Word gets around, and you don't strike me as the hero type. Besides, he's building a place in Montparnasse to keep her."

"That kid thinks she's going to London."

"Guess you better start minding your own fucking business."

FRANCES HEENAN CAME TO BRICKTOP'S as part of her 1936 European tour.

"But you can call me Peaches," she told the crowded club. "Even the *New York Daily News* does." Then she waved to the musicians behind her, cleared her throat, and began singing about her love being *très fort* and if her French was better, she'd say more, darling.

"Can't carry a tune," said Bricky at the bar, picking a piece of tobacco off her tooth. "Or dance."

Rain had never heard of her.

"Big scandal in New York, 'bout ten years ago. Married Daddy Browning, millionaire three times her age. She was only sixteen. Papers said he kept a pet goose in the bedroom." Bricky exhaled a long blue puff of smoke, shaking her head at the eccentricities of the rich and those who want to be. "No surprise it didn't end well. She tried to divorce him after a few months and didn't get a penny. But you know me. I'm a sucker for a hard-luck story. Poor kid. She's got moxie, though. And she does pack 'em in."

Rain wasn't listening to anything anymore but the pounding, throbbing in his ears. After all this time, there she was. Casually stepping through the leather curtains, laughing with that gap-tooth smile. Her pink gown slithered across the red carpet and a white rabbit stole wrapped her bare shoulders. Her hair glittered, at least to Rain it did, and satin gloves covered her arms up to her elbows.

"You okay, honey?" Bricky looked beyond Peaches to the group being seated by the dance floor. "Friend of yours?"

Rain pulled at his collar, managed to nod. "Long time ago."

"English? Yeah, thought so. You can always tell the English. Better manners, but no sense of style. I mean, pink for Christ's sake."

Bricky leaned across the bar and told the barman, Thomas, to send over a bottle of champagne, on the house. Not the good stuff, mind you.

"Your lady friend keeps interesting company," Bricky said. "That man she's with, Pierre Gallard. He's a big chief in the French war ministry. Used to come in here a lot. Haven't seen him for a while."

The waiter delivered the bottle to Lily's table, and then nodded to the bar. Lily looked surprised, maybe even confused, then she smiled in a way that Rain thought perhaps she had not for some time. The narrow little man beside her with the neat, razored moustache appeared put upon by the gesture.

"Whatever that gal did to you, she's still doing it. Better get over there and say hello."

Rain thought he felt Bricky's hand give his back a gentle nudge as he stepped onto the empty dance floor in front of a gyrating Peaches.

"Daddy used to take me out to Atlantic City in nothing but a bathing suit." Peaches was doing a soft-shoe shuffle. "And me just a girl." She tried to hide her face demurely behind her upraised hand. "A very chilly girl, at that."

The crowd laughed along as Rain reached Lily's table.

"You dear old thing. Is it really you?"

She reached for his hand, but Pierre intercepted. "And who is this?"

Lily kept her smile and only Rain noticed that a light went off inside under the thick makeup.

"Why, this is, our, my—"

"I was madam's gardener. In England."

Pierre tapped a cigarette out of his case. "Gardener, eh? In a monkey suit at Bricktop's. What a world. Perhaps he could do something for us."

Lily's eyes never left Rain's. "Oh, yes, you must. Say you will."

"Of course if your man here has other work, we'd understand. Wouldn't we, *mon cher.*"

"You must come to visit us." Lily glanced at Pierre. "For the garden. You know I've been going on about it forever."

Pierre nodded with eyes half open, clearly bored with the reunion.

Lily persisted. "We're at 32 rue de Fleurus. Tomorrow? Say you will come to see me tomorrow."

Dancing girls wearing rolled-downed tights and satin top hats sent Peaches skipping from the stage with a salute.

"Promise? Rue de Fleurus. You will remember?"

RAIN RATTLED THE IRON BARS, but did not open the gate. Years of worry, nights of drowning dreams, days of aimless wandering. Clinging to an idea of her, exalted and guarded and forgiven. Life had given him only a crumb of love, but unlike the fiery passions of others he witnessed nightly at Bricktop's, his morsel of a dream would at least not grow old or fade or look haggard in the morning. Maybe he was better off alone, yes, and lonely, with Lily remaining that girl stuck in the mud who'd collected hearts from all she knew. *I have loved, and that's enough. Walk away.* If he were to get involved again now she would surely need him, and he would let her take whatever bits of heart he had left to give. If he stepped through this gate, whatever was to come, he was sure he would forever forfeit his chance to be free of her.

"I thought it was you out there," she said brightly, hurriedly.

He followed her past the sitting rooms and through to the walled court, trailing her floral fragrance. The grass was lined with boxwoods in need of a clip, and a graciously overgrown linden shaded more than its fair share of the garden.

"It's not—" She stopped before pronouncing the name. *Walling.*

Lily offered Rain a seat on one of the delicately uncomfortable wrought iron chairs. The legs sank into the ground when he sat.

"No, it's nice. Peaceful."

No amount of powder would conceal the purple bruise just under her jaw.

"I can't believe it. My darling thing, here with me." Her hands knotted together nervously and she wondered about tea. Did he still drink tea? "Do you know, how he is?"

"I heard he sailed for Cape Town after losing Walling. Died a few years later. Cancer, or something."

Lily's hands shook as she poured the tea, so much so that Rain took the pot from her and finished. The cups were small and Rain's fingers were big.

"Shall I get you a proper mug?"

Lily's smile kept fleeing. The sudden rustling of the linden behind them seemed to be saying *Get on with it.*

"They never found him, you know. Euan I mean."

"I'd wondered," she said in a way that made Rain wonder if in fact she had. Lily flattened her hands on her lap. "It really is good to see you again."

"Andrew kept Walling as long as he could. For you."

"And you see, Pierre has a position with the government. We're well taken care of."

She did not want to talk about the past.

"Are you happy?"

Of course she was, what a question, and Rain knew instantly that she wasn't.

The street door opened and from inside the passageway, Rain heard automobiles pass on the street and a woman speaking French, something about a *chat* in the park and *mademoiselle* was most upset she could not bring it home and keep it. Lily stood, but before she could close the garden door, a smiling Frenchwoman chasing after a child burst upon them.

"*Madame, excusez-moi.*"

Man and child stared at one another awkwardly. The child, round and red in the face, with big eyes and black hair, part Lily, but not Pierre, clung to her nurse, the cat in the park now all but forgotten.

"No, it's all right," said Lily. She introduced her daughter, Nora, then sent her away with the nurse.

"Now you see why I did not return, and why I was so insistent to see you."

All Rain saw was the girl, carrying away shattered bits of his boyish dream as she climbed the stairs. Husbands were just an accoutrement for Lily, but a child?

"Pierre must be very happy," he could all but whisper.

"Nora is not his."

*Oh.*

"Can't you see? She's your daughter."

Rain wished he'd taken the offer of a mug. The teacup, gripped so tightly in his hand, was bound to shatter, cut his hands to pieces, leave him lying under the linden dying from blood loss just when his story was getting good.

"Forgive me. I shouldn't have told you like this, but I was here in Paris when I knew—"

"And she's mine? You're sure?"

"Well...yes. What are you saying?" she asked angrily. "Do you think I'm lying?"

"What about the major?" he asked. *What about Euan?* he thought.

"Andrew...couldn't give me children. He blamed the war, and before you ask, no, he never knew about her. He was being piggy about a divorce or giving me a living. It was the last thing he needed to find out. Pierre came along, gave me a home, no questions." It all sounded so perfectly reasonable. She laughed. "What was I to do? I mean, it's not like *you* could have."

He barely felt the sting of her words, or how any thought of how he might feel had been left out of them. Instead he wondered, *My daughter?*

But there was Lily kneeling before him, taking his hands into hers. "You should know I don't blame you. You were very drunk and I was so upset by him—"

"Who?"

Lily dropped his hands and backed away. "Andrew, of course. He was very unkind to me that night. Accused me of terrible things. Anyhow, you were very sweet and gentle. We both had too much to drink."

Lily's hands trembled as she reached for a cigarette.

"I know I shouldn't speak ill of the dead, but Andrew was a vindictive man, you have no idea, no idea at all what he was capable of. I saved you, really, by not telling him. Everything you had came from him. At the very least, he'd dismiss you, you'd have had nothing, and where would that have left us all?" She looked searchingly at Rain's face, which remained still, impassive, confused.

*But Nora's beautiful...how can she be mine?*

"Promise me you won't say anything. Pierre is a very proud man. I told him her father was dead. He wouldn't take kindly to knowing about you, and well, you really can't provide for us, can you? It's not like we loved each other. I wanted to thank you for saving me that night—and it just happened. We'd both been drinking. Sometimes I think I drink too much."

Rain stood, needing to be free of the uncomfortable metal chair, her hands, the smell of her, the small confines of this garden.

"Please, say something. Anything. Just don't hate me."

Until that moment, Rain hadn't thought that possible.

THEY SAILED INTO UNCHARTED water warily. Nora, eyes wide and black and penetrating, lips pressed tightly together, refusing to cry. Rain, hurt and sad and bewildered, knowing only that the child changed everything. Forever. Maybe this was how Lily wouldn't matter so much anymore.

"Shall we be friends?" Rain asked.

"You have a very naughty face," Nora said.

NORA WOULD NOT PRACTICE HER VERBS, but what could be done? No one cared. Monsieur worked long and late and the mother, according to the nurse, was no better than a child herself. Dangle a sparkly bauble or trip to the theatre in front of her, and out she went. For all her criticism, the nurse, when she saw that Rain was easily coerced into watching over Nora while on his hands and knees in the garden, wasn't above earning her wages by reading lurid novels up in her room with a glass of Pierre's sherry.

For Nora's dollhouse, Rain created ornately dressed ladies from overturned pink and yellow hollyhock blossoms, each carrying a bouquet of white spirea. But Nora had to touch them carefully or he'd have to make new ones and his thumbs were very big for such dainty work. "And see, these ones, they're called cornflowers."

"*Bleuet*," said Nora.

"Your grandmother used to grow them. She'd hang them to dry over my bed so when it got very cold in the winter my brothers and I could reach up like this, and run our fingers through summer."

He handed a blue flower to Nora who quickly tore it apart.

Rain stomped around the garden like he was a bear. "Did you eat my flower?"

They both laughed.

"Now this one, this is a lily. Can you say lily *en française*? That's your mother's name too. See, don't they smell pretty?"

On sunny days he'd take her on his shoulders to the nearby park where they'd feed the pigeons so that *épaules!* soon became her demand for her preferred mode of transportation. At the end of each day together, before Rain left, he'd get down on his knees and quietly, so that no one else could hear, ask Nora: *qui est votre meilleur ami?* She would touch the small hollow at the base of his throat and throw her arms about his neck.

Nora was usually so tired after a day with him that she went right to sleep, running after the three little ducks, *quack, quack, quack,* as Rain had taught her.

"You're an angel," Lily told him. She was not cut out to be a mother, she said, and Pierre, he demanded quiet after a long day.

"I KNOW SHE'S A FRIEND of yours, honey, but I know the signs."

Bricky was eyeing Lily and Pierre and the group of Germans they were entertaining. Lily told Rain that they had something to do with armaments, though she was never very good at details.

"Gloves covering her arms, the way she's got her hair brushed over that eye. No amount of makeup is hiding those bruises."

"She told me she fell horseback riding."

"Honey, no one rides in Paris. Take my advice. Stay away. Get between a man doing that to a woman, you'll come out the worse for it. And she won't thank you."

THE ACTRESS WITH LONG CURLED hair pursed her lips suggestively around a cigarette. "He's a fucking genius, Irene. I'm telling you, get David to hire him." She sounded deeper, raspier than a man.

Bricky told everyone at the table to shut up. She was trying to convince some singer from New York to give up a song.

"Jesus Christ, Bricky, darling, if I have to listen to 'Old Man River' one more time, I'm going to stick my fingers down my throat and bring up everything! Right here on your table."

The woman sitting on the other side of the raspy woman, Irene Selznick, felt the need to apologize by way of explaining that her friend Tula was very drunk.

"About to get drunker, but not before I get you to hire this good man. What's your name?" Tula thumped Rain on the chest.

"Irene and her husband got themselves one of those...you know, big places with a turret thingamajig."

"Chateau?"

"That's it. Quaint, if you're into old shit. Left over from when they cut people's heads off around here. But big. You know what I mean. Garden hasn't had a trim since the war."

"We've only leased the place, dear, and we're heading back to the States day after tomorrow. David's got his hands on that book and you know what he's like. Chafing at the bit to start filming."

"I know! I've read it, and Irene, Scarlett's the perfect role for me. Everyone in New York says so."

The Hollywood producer's wife, who Bricky whispered to Rain was a more stylish version of Wallis Simpson, but unfortunately Jewish, said every actress in Hollywood thought they were perfect for the role.

"Irene, darling, no matter. But listen, I hear this man changed some garden over in Italy, every fucking day. Go on, tell 'em, buddy."

"England."

Huh?

"The garden was in Yorkshire."

"Where the fuck is that?"

"Sailing, Tula, day after tomorrow," said Irene.

"He can do you a new garden tonight, can't you?"

Irene told her husband as he sat down and knocked out a cigarette from his case that Tula was insisting Rain was a wizard with a hoe.

"You don't look like one." Rain offered the man a light. "But what do I know? The closest I've ever got to a garden is that piece with Dietrich."

Everyone at the table laughed. Rain managed a smile. He had no idea what they were talking about.

"I'm telling you, David, because that wife of yours is deaf, *hire* the man. He's a fucking genius."

"So everyone has heard you say."

"Marjorie got me onto him. You remember my dear friend Marjorie Winston, from that...you know, that place we were all at. Oh, Christ, Irene, where was it?"

"Palm Springs?"

"Yes! She read in a magazine he could put in a new garden every day."

"Really?"

Rain insisted the story was somewhat overtold, and anyway, he was very busy in Paris. He still had Bricktop's to take care of.

"If I know Bricky, you're working for watered-down beer."

She'd been good to him. Rain owed her.

"Darling, have you any idea what she's pulling in here tonight alone? She charges a hundred fucking francs for a bottle of watered-down piss."

"You really that good a gardener?" the producer asked.

"David, why won't you listen to me? He's a fucking genius. And besides, look at him. It's not like you'd ever have to worry about Irene having an affair with the help."

"Jesus, Tula—"

"Fatty Arbuckle. That's who he reminds me of, Irene. Been bothering me, that." Taking hold of Rain's arm, she added, "Darling, you remind me of Fatty Arbuckle."

"Oh, Father never cared for Fatty," Irene said. "MGM wouldn't touch him. You know, you look more like that fellow from Tula's last picture. What was his name? Charlie Laughton."

"A swine. Don't mention that fiend's name to me. Didn't bathe once the whole time." Tula snapped her fingers for another drink.

David tapped Rain on the arm. "I can't figure out if Tula's a fan of yours or not."

"I know," said the actress, fumbling with her lighter. "David, put him in the movies!"

Rain laughed nervously as he looked for an escape.

"No, darling, he can do it," said Tula to him, leaning in close. "He's David Selznick. You must have seen his movies?"

Rain hadn't, but no one seemed to care what he was thinking.

"All right, all right. Pardon me! David *O.* Selznick. Sounds less Jewish these days, all things considered." Tula nodded to the table of Germans sitting with Lily and Pierre and pulled a face.

"Tula, you know I don't do horror flicks," said the producer.

"Not *in* them, David, you idiot. Making your film gardens. You could use him, honey, I've seen your sets."

Bricky finally managed to clear the floor and shushed everyone because she'd got Paul Robeson to sing.

"Listen." David took a card out of his pocket and slipped it towards Rain. "Tallulah's a mouthy drunk, but I do trust her instincts. If what she says is true, I've got something big coming up. Could use someone like you."

When Rain came round to the throbbing headache, he found Bricky stitching up the gash on his forehead.

"Looks like you ought to be used to this. Can't say my stitching is going to be so fine, though."

*Oh, Jesus.*

"Found you lying in the doorway."

Coming home. The light out over the stairs. He'd just inserted the key into the door. The memory of what came next was as bad as the pain.

"You see who did this?"

"He was waiting down the hall. Short guy. Kinda bulky."

Only man he'd ever seen who had a face worse than his.

"Lardet." Bricky stopped with the needle. "I warned you."

Rain winced as she returned to the matter of his face. "You sure you know what you're doing?"

"You're not the first pretty face I've stitched up."

"Ouch. Christ!"

"Told you not to cross him," said Bricky.

"How did I do that?"

"His girl ran off. You didn't know?"

"I haven't seen her. Not since he took her."

"She didn't contact you?"

"No."

"Doesn't matter. Tonight was Lardet's way of saying he doesn't want you around."

"But I didn't do anything to that girl."

"You were *nice* to that girl."

Rain tried to sit up, but Bricky pushed him back so she could finish the stitching.

"I'm not going anywhere. I can't."

"Because of that bleached blonde you moon over every night out there? You stay in Paris, you'll end up floating in the Seine. You go to her, you bring Lardet to her door. And he already knows where you live."

Bricky snipped the thread with scissors. "Honey, I hate to lose you, but you're going to get on the train tonight and the boat to America in the morning. I already told that movie producer you'd take his offer."

*Magnolia grandiflora*

# 1937

The young woman waiting on the Los Angeles railway platform stood defiant amidst the chaos.

"Are you Miss Hepner?" Rain set down his small suitcase and swabbed the sweat beading on his forehead. His back ached from days on the train.

"Helen'll do just fine." She thrust out her hand and took Rain's. "Gee, mister, what happened to your face?" She didn't wait for a reply as she took his suitcase and led him through the crowd. "Oh, don't mind me, I'm only asking what everyone's going to want to know. Good trip?"

She spoke loudly and rapidly, like someone born to a large family who'd had to fight for every word and mouthful. Hadn't he come all the way from Paris? She was going there some-day, London too. Did he believe what everyone was saying about another war coming? Leave it to those dirty Germans. When she was growing up, there was a kid in school with a German-sounding name. Martin or Mueller or something. Real piece of work. Probably one of those, you know, Nazi spies now. Maybe Rain could recommend some place to stay over there. In Paris obviously. Not too expensive, but with clean sheets and food like she ate here. Helen had dreams, you see, and lots of them.

The young woman walked fast and Rain better keep up.

"You don't sound French," she said.

"I'm not."

"Don't sound very English either, not like the posh ones. I just love Merle Oberon, seen all her movies. I hear that you're some famous European landscaper."

Hardly that, and he'd not even be in California if it weren't for a very drunk Tallulah Bankhead.

"That so? What *have* you done?"

In his nervous defense, and Rain couldn't believe he mentioned it, he referenced that hateful mess of a story in *Town & Country*, though it was years ago.

"Which article? My aunt reads every copy."

"Walling. House in Yorkshire."

"That so?" Helen stopped her forced march and turned on Rain. "Don't mind telling you, mister, my aunts expect someone who knows what they're doing to work on this movie."

"I'm not working for you?"

"Jeepers! I just drive the truck and type the letters. Mostly I like to drive. Nope, you work for them, and they work for Mr. Selznick."

Helen led the way out of the station and slipped into the driver's seat of the wood-panelled truck, where she sat on a phone book.

"Can't see over the hood without it," she said, shifting into gear. "Drop you off at the Ardmore Hotel. Nothing fancy but it's clean and you can rent by the month until you get settled. I guess that's if they keep you around."

Mr. Selznick's secretary had made the arrangements, she continued as they pulled onto the road, so he wasn't to blame

Helen if the place had bugs. She'd had her first drink there when she turned twenty-one. Everyone knew Joan Crawford got drunk there once and danced the Charleston on top of the piano.

"Studio tomorrow," she added, pulling under the faded canary-green awning. "Pick you up at ten."

RAIN SLID INTO THE SEAT beside Helen the next morning, and she tossed him a Thermos full of hot coffee.

"Don't know if you even drink coffee over there in France, but figured you could use some. Sleep well?"

Not at all, but sure, he said, about the coffee. "Where are the others?"

"Up early. Over in Chatsworth in the valley. Florence is doing a movie about some Chinese guy for Mr. Thalberg. She wanted to check on the crew flooding the rice paddies this morning with a water truck. Don't worry, she'll be back in time for your meeting."

"Florence is your aunt?"

"Not really. It's 'cause she's with my Aunt Lucile, so she's like my aunt, too." Helen gripped the wheel, then waved her finger in Rain's face. "Say, you got a problem with that? Because if you do, I better not know about it."

Not Rain. He'd been living in Paris.

He glanced at Los Angeles out the window of the truck. Sprawling. Sunny. Palm trees. Nora-less. Lily-less. Movie theatre in the shape of a sphinx. Restaurant wearing a top hat.

"Since you didn't ask, I came to help out in the office when Mr. Selznick sent Florence to Africa for *The Garden of Allah.* She's the one with the good ideas, but she got the worst case of the scoots over there. Aunt Lucile can hold onto a buck tighter than a Jew. You see that movie?"

Rain shook his head.

"Too many sad close-ups for me. I like action. Last year she did *Romeo and Juliet* so I got to meet Leslie Howard. Nice guy, not my cat's meow though if you catch my meaning." She made like her wrist had gone limp. "Clark Gable. Now there's a tall, cool drink of delicious."

The sort of men all women wanted, Lily included. Handsome. Rugged. *Not me.*

"Work in movies long? Your aunt and Florence?"

"Florence did up Mr. Selznick's place in Beverly Hills, he liked it and she helped him out with making Africa look like Africa. Now they're working on *The Good Earth.* Sometimes they do gardens for movie stars. More money than brains, that bunch. Think nothing of spending hundreds of thousands 'cause they want a mountaintop carved out for their new villa with full-grown trees and ivy terraces, dancing nymphs looking like they've been spitting water for centuries. And you know what? One flop and up goes the For Sale sign. Guess that's why you're here all the way from France."

"Huh?"

"*Gone With the Wind,* silly. Haven't you heard? Everyone's reading it. Aunt Lucile says Mr. Selznick got the rights for fifty thousand. Imagine. For a book. I just bet that's what this meeting's about."

"You think so?"

"He wants you to work on the film, mark my words."

"But I don't know anything about movies."

"Don't tell him that, for heaven's sake. Besides, Florence does. Could be exciting, don't you think?"

"You want to be an actress?"

"Do I look like the kind of gal that starves on cucumber water and diet pills? No sir. Besides, I'd have to get my nose fixed and I hate hospitals. I'm a good secretary and not many girls get to drive a truck around the lots. Suits me fine until some swell guy sweeps me off my feet and gives me a couple of kids."

Rain forced himself to smile.

"Sorry. My mother says I talk too much without thinking. You married there, fella?"

Rain smiled wanly and wondered, how was he ever going to put up with this girl?

"Here we are." Helen turned the truck through the gates at Selznick International. She honked the horn at the set dressers carrying a spinning wheel and a roast turkey made out of papier mâché from one of the sound stages. "Land o'happily-ever-after. I'll wait in the truck."


RAIN FELT LIKE A FRAUD sitting between Florence Yoch and Lucile Council, across an enormous desk from David O. Selznick. Both women wore trousers and buttoned-up blouses. Florence styled her abundant hair in a turn-of-the-century Gibson. The impenetrable Lucile kept her arms folded resolutely across her chest.

"We're going to make the most expensive movie in Hollywood history," Selznick said, sliding that biblical-sized novel across his desk and looking at all three of them like they had just won the Irish Sweepstakes.

Rain felt nauseous.

What did he know about making movies? He'd only ever seen one; a grainy black-and-white he took Nora to one rainy afternoon. The actors chased each other around and spoke French so he understood little, but everyone ended up with a pie in the face. Nora laughed. His Nora. He wondered what she was doing right at that moment. Was she feeding pigeons at the park? Was she conjugating her verbs? How soon would she forget him? They forget things so easily when they're young. He knew he'd get nothing from Lily in the way of letters. Dear Lily, so selfish and self-absorbed she wouldn't even hear the tread of Nazi boots on her own porch.

"YOU CAN DO ANYTHING IF you can do this."

Helen meant changing the gardens at Walling. Florence had found the yellowing *Town & Country* magazine for her to read on the plane. "You'd think this guy in all the pictures did the work. How come you're not here?"

Florence leaned into the aisle from her seat and had a look. "What's he doing now?"

Of course, Helen would want to know about Euan. What woman didn't? It always surprised him, that hard ball of anger that still rose from the pit of his stomach, leaving him with the bitter aftertaste of guilt. Even from those jaundiced pages there was no denying his good looks. His charm, which exuded even from a dry old page, and which had swooped Lily out of her marriage and into a treacherous birchbark canoe. *He's dead. Drowned. They never found the body.*

But Rain just said he'd lost touch.

And it wasn't the same thing, he wanted to argue. Rearranging a few plants every night did not compare with visually interpreting a book that, from what Rain understood, had become a national obsession, every detail debated in newspapers and fan magazines. Politicians even waded in. Especially since Selznick had started his countrywide search for his leading lady.

"From what I've seen, no one in the business really knows how to make a movie, so don't worry. There's no how-to book. It's all on a kiss and a prayer and you've got Florence to help. You really don't have much room in that seat, do you?"

The seat belt was too tight. Outside the tiny oval window, Rain could see the propellers on the DC-3 spinning. Because he'd never flown before, Florence and Helen insisted he get one of the window seats. No point in missing the fun in takeoffs and landings, they'd said.

"I heard one Scarlett popped out of an oversized plywood book wearing a hoop skirt and holding a handful of magnolia blossoms," said Helen. "At the studio gates. Insisted she *was* Scarlett because she'd been born in the same Georgia county."

This trip to Atlanta was for research. Lucile was staying behind in Los Angeles to carry on with other commissions while Helen mapped out routes around the southern countryside so Florence and Rain could get a visual idea of the landscape. But Rain didn't know that the trip meant flying across the country in a soup-can-like cabin, wedged into a seat that felt like it was designed for a child, with no air to breathe. He felt queasy, feverish, and was sweating in a most ungentlemanly fashion.

"Wiggle your toes. Gets the blood circulating," said Helen knowingly.

She'd flown to San Diego so she considered herself an ace, but she was not the size of Rain and for her, wiggling her toes was an option. When they flew into the first of the bumps and dips, she smiled and said "Relax, just turbulence." Maybe Rain needed something to eat, sandwiches and soup along with coffee. Helen was now nose deep in a copy of *Photoplay*, her hand over her mouth as she read how Jean Harlow had died of uremic poisoning. Florence was jotting notes in the margin of Mitchell's ponderous novel.

*Maybe if I lean back, close my eyes, try to sleep, this will pass.* But the nausea only worsened, as did the torrent of sweat running down his face. *Turbulence be damned.* He undid the seat belt that was almost cutting him in half.

When he next opened his eyes, the first thing he saw was the propeller. It wasn't turning.

"It's okay, we've landed," Helen said in a calm whisper. She held his hand; his other gripped a linen napkin so tightly his fingers had gone numb. "Some tea and toast. That's what you need. Settles your bowels right down."

Over her shoulder stood a man in a double-breasted suit, who also examined Rain closely. "I think he'll be fine now, miss," he said.

"Are you sure?"

He shrugged lightly. "Passed out from motion sickness. Happens much more than you think."

Helen thanked the man.

"Good thing the doc was on the flight. You had us worried. I thought you were having a seizure."

Rain felt wet, as if he'd sweat through his shirt and suit jacket.

Florence got up out of her seat to survey the damage. "Oh, dear. Looks like lunch came up."

THE MAYOR OF ATLANTA, along with several women from the Daughters of the Confederacy and a child staggering under a bushel of roses, waited for them on the tarmac. From the look on the mayor's face, Rain wished he'd changed his shirt.

"I didn't think anyone knew we were coming."

Florence looked resigned. Mr. Selznick, miss an opportunity for some free publicity?

Mayor Hartsfield welcomed them to the city, saying that he had heard they were scouting locations and wished to offer the assistance of the Daughters. Would Miss Yoch and Rain and the young lady be available for dinner that evening at City Hall?

"Why not?" Helen said as she drove them away from the airport. "Kinda fun letting them treat us like movie stars."

"But we're not. We're here to work," said Florence. She insisted they forego the formalities and get to the hotel so Rain could bathe and change.

In the morning, Helen waited with the car and an arm full of maps. Although they'd been offered a driver, Helen wasn't giving up an opportunity to burn rubber, as she put it, on southern roads.

"Not like driving in Los Angeles," she shrilled happily as they bounced over the clay ruts. When she wasn't driving, Helen haggled prices with hotel clerks, filled petrol cans she kept in the hired car, and in the evening, typed letters reporting back to Mr. Selznick in California. Over eggs and toast in the morning, she organized the research sketches, and then with a Thermos of coffee and a copy of *Gone With the Wind* in hand, knocked on homeowners' doors to ask, would they mind if Florence and Rain walked through your pasture to have a look at some honest-to-goodness real southern flowers?

RAIN FIRST THOUGHT HE SAW Nora holding a man's hand outside a bookstore in Marietta. Then she was in a bus window in Fairburn. She pumped her legs through a tire hung from a tree in a fenced yard in Jonesboro. Sometimes he saw just her face, or glimpsed her only on the lift of an eyelid, or the crease of a frown. He mailed letters, dolls, and stuffed dogs to her. Even candy. Spent a fortune in cables. They never came back undelivered, but nor did any note of thanks reach him. Maybe Pierre and Lily no longer lived on the rue de Fleurus. Then how would he find her?

"Sure, I'll stop in and ask if there's anything for you at the telegraph office. Again," said Helen. "Because it's not like I haven't got anything better to do. But if you ask me, better spend some time reading that book you're making the movie about. Take your mind off the worry. 'Course, why bother reading a thousand pages when you can flip to the end and find out what happens. Won't tell ya how, but she had it coming."

The ever-darkening news from Europe didn't help. Helen said Rain shouldn't waste money on newspapers. Too depressing. The krauts, the frogs, the limeys, who cared what mischief they got up to, and besides, that was far way. Didn't President Roosevelt say they weren't getting involved in any European squabble? In a few more days they'd be flying back to Los Angeles. Don't get much farther away from a war than that.

But Germany was flexing muscles, impatiently. Rain was anxious for news, any news. He hated reading about the treatment of the Jews, but he couldn't seem to stop himself. His face had been the product of the war to end all wars. How could this be happening again, only a handful of years later? Yet it seemed it was so. Every day columnists and foreign reporters filed the same story that nobody wanted to read. Germany was rearming. Paris, and Lily and Nora, his Nora, were only five hundred miles from Berlin.

In rubber galoshes, Florence and Rain picked their way through the swamp maples clinging to the steaming stream, their faces covered in bug netting. The evening's first indolent fireflies seemed not to care how easily they could be dinner for the catfish just below the surface. Helen waited back in the car listening to the radio. "Not gettin' paid to get eaten alive," she had said.

"Don't mind Helen," said Florence, her hand trailing through the low-hanging leaves. "She likes to make out she's a hard apple, but really, she's one of the kindest souls I know. I believe she's quite taken with you."

Rain had risen in Florence's estimation when she had caught him sketching during their days hiking through wet fields searching for rundown ruins of abandoned farmhouses. Florence's own sketchbook was filled with notes and drawings of Cape Jasmine gardenias, iron oaks, dogwood, mimosa, and Maréchal Niel roses. She was delighted to share. When Florence smiled, she didn't look so much like a woman trying to look like a man.

"We're going to have a battle with Mr. Selznick," she said. "He'll want Greek columns and cotton fields in every shot."

"Mostly peanut farms around here."

"Everyone who's read the book will want them too."

"Does it matter? It's a movie."

"It matters very much. Movies aren't just for eating popcorn in a dark theatre and watching beautiful people and beautiful places. It's about what happens to you here." She tapped Rain's chest. "How they make you feel. How they make you *want* to feel. The garden may only take up a few minutes on the screen, seconds even, but more often than not, it's just as important as the actors, only the director will never say. Sometimes the director doesn't even know. Consider this your first formal lesson about what we do."

From the car radio, Fred Astaire proclaimed that he wasn't letting anyone take anything away from him. The rolled up windows must have made the inside too hot for Helen, for now they were down and her bare feet dangled outside as mosquito fodder.

Florence flipped opened her sketchbook and with a few scratching pencil marks, drew steps to a placid canal lorded over by cypresses, the wall of the Capulet house in behind. Her garden for *Romeo and Juliet*.

"Movie gardens aren't just something pretty in the background. Plants are the silent words, the mood, the emotion connecting the audience with the actor."

Florence sketched in more trees, one of them slightly askew.

"The off-angle tree, or a wall a few degrees out of alignment, makes things look worn by time. Very important in a set that must look old. Flowering fruit trees, or annuals in pots, now that's spring, seasonal, youth. Here, put a shrub at the corner of this building and it looks like it's the only thing holding the place up. Doesn't that make you feel unsettled? Like the whole structure could come crashing down. Same idea for a bush darkening out a wall like a secret door."

Florence flipped a page and drew an obelisk.

"Cemetery, right? Put this up front in your garden, and I guarantee you everyone in the audience is thinking about death, a funeral, a burial, or maybe just an ending, but they got there without anyone saying a word. And here's a great trick if you want to heighten the illusion of distance." She drew a few swift lines. "Plant a row of trees with a curve, each tree slightly lower than the one in front. Put a tree by itself in a field, you're thinking loneliness. Lots of heavy vines hide a mystery. If you want the audience to be thinking about the past, try clusters of mature yews broken here and there by a fruit tree. Rows of clipped boxwood mean order, they're calming. And use architecture for tradition. For a shot with a single element, like this"—Florence sketched a broken arch—"your movie's about a great, lasting, but doomed romance."

Rain was impressed. More so, he understood. "If anyone can get Selznick to give up the Greek columns, it's you."

Florence raised a skeptical eyebrow. "He's a producer, so it's about what people want because it's about the tickets they'll buy. And his father-in-law is Louis B. Mayer. Still, Mr. Selznick's different. He's one of the few in Hollywood who's an artist in his own right. When I explain to him that his concept for Tara is romantic codswallop, he'll see sense, eventually. Mr. Selznick wants this picture to be a classic. A masterpiece. No, our real challenge is going to be finding plants in California that can mimic what we see here."

"But who'll know the difference?"

"You and me."

PRINCIPAL FILMING ON THE MOVIE was still months away when they returned from Atlanta, but with Florence suggesting it'd be a good idea to get some practical experience, Selznick got Rain work on Sam Goldwyn's *Wuthering Heights*. Rain's job was to fill a set in a southern California valley with heather.

"But he won't use the right kind," Rain complained to Helen over coffee in the commissary.

The director, Bill Wyler, wanted to know how many kinds of heather there could possibly be.

Rain knew; he'd lived in Yorkshire and the heather Wyler wanted was wrong, he grumbled. "High as a bush."

Wyler didn't care. Americans wouldn't know the difference. Besides, the script called for Heathcliff to fill Cathy's arms with heather. So goddammit! Fill them! That piddly stuff Rain was going on about was as photographic as dustballs.

Rain felt that they were lying to the audience, and so he hated working on the movie—but he did manage to get Helen a lunch with Merle Oberon. The usually talkative young woman wasn't able to get a word out over her lunch of macaroni and cheese.

More enjoyable was the work outside of the studio that Florence put his way. The demand for her gardens was more than she and Lucile could meet, so Florence was only too happy to recommend Rain. Here he shone. His use of Walling's theatrics carried over easily into the gardens he designed in Los

Angeles, for what took an audience's breath away, or helped move them to tears during a handful of seconds on film, was just what movie folks wanted in their backyards to dazzle cocktail guests.

ON RAIN'S FIRST VISIT to Forty Acres, the Culver City back lot where the art director, Lyle Wheeler, was overseeing the construction of the set for Scarlett O'Hara's Tara plantation, he could see Florence had won. No Greek columns in sight.

"It was quite the fight," her eyebrows rose as she recounted the victory to Rain. "He really was partial to them."

"How did you convince him?"

"Sent Lyle's original sketch with Corinthian columns to the author. Fort Sumter all over again. South won this round."

Already the plywood framing for the house's front was in place.

"What's our budget?" Rain asked.

"Sixteen thousand."

"That much for a film?"

"For the house. We've got another ten thousand to do Twelve Oaks and the Butler place in Atlanta. And here, you'd better read this." She handed him Mr. Selznick's five-page memo instructing Florence and Rain not to drape everything in Spanish moss.

"Any ideas where we can get a couple of giant magnolias?"

Rain knew of several just outside of the city. He'd come across them one day when he and Helen had been looking for trees for a client.

"Too far. We'd never get them here, and they'd be dead in days. We've got to keep them alive for weeks."

But at Bon Sauveur and at Walling, Rain had successfully moved mature trees.

Rain impressed Florence with his accounts of trenches and boxed roots, and soon the magnolias were trucked back to the set, hoisted by cranes into place, and framed with a scattering of shrubs and vines much like the ones they'd found strangling antebellum ruins in Georgia. Florence planted a fluted crape myrtle on one side of Tara's porch, balanced with ivy that took her a week to thread to her liking along the faux brick.

For oaks, Rain saw to the dressing of telephone poles, framed with chicken wire and covered in plaster. Wires were strung from the tops of these poles to the roof of the house facade. From these, he dropped lengths of artificial leaves so the cameras could catch foreground shadows. Around the house Helen helped him plant trees similar to dogwood, and saw to it that blossoms, handmade in the Property Department, were carefully tied to the branches.

As Rain waved directions to a bulldozer cutting a rough road into a low hill near the porch of the plantation house, he remembered Lily and Walling and that look of delight she wore the first time they had transformed the garden.

As he crawled about the freshly turfed mound under the magnolia, placing sunken pots of flowers that would have to be replaced often during the course of filming, Rain hoped that Nora's tenth birthday had ponies and carousels and maybe even a clown.

And on that last summer day when Helen complained about trying to tie those nasty and foul-smelling peacocks to stakes so they wouldn't wander off camera while Vivien Leigh sat on the porch and complained about war war war, England declared it on Germany.

*Centaurea cyanus*

# 1940

The letter arrived in February with a six-week-old postmark. Rain had spent the day in Montecito where he was overseeing the construction of Mrs. Vroman's exedra: square, unadorned columns with plain benches surrounding a low-set fountain and a stacked wall, capped with a row of white-painted bricks holding back a curtain of Monterey cypress, rose oleander, and the toothy-white blossoms of Clematis armandii.

More work than Rain could manage came his way these days, and while the studios still clamoured after his talents, he was relieved that financially he could say no. Digging up decades-old trees for a few seconds of film only to let them die left Rain feeling like he had blood on his hands. Only another gardener could understand that, and Florence had been gracious when they amicably parted ways after *Gone With the Wind* was finished.

Rain rented a down-on-its-luck three-bedroom bungalow with board and batten siding in East San Gabriel. An empty pool sat as a cracked aquamarine hole in a backyard overgrown with bushes where neighbours left terse notes in the mailbox about unmowed grass. Helen had helped him furnish the place from thrift shops with a desk, a wobbly card table, a couple of mismatched chairs, and a narrow and unforgiving bed that looked suspiciously military and squealed like an old cat when he crawled in. After that, Rain expected not to see the young woman again, and so he was surprised when she arrived at his door the next morning, with her usual Thermos full of coffee and a rhubarb pie. The only thing she could find in the nearby market that would do for breakfast. She quickly assured him that Florence and Lucile could get along just fine without her and, looking around the sparsely furnished bedroom that Rain planned to use for an office, it appeared he could not.

"It came yesterday. From France. Care of the studio." Helen meant the letter she held out to him. "Mr. Selznick's secretary sent it over."

Rain was standing in the doorway, the mud on his denim coveralls having dried to clay patches, wearing an oversized straw hat to battle against the hot California sun.

"You okay?"

Rain managed to nod his head, or at least he thought he did, and let Helen place the letter into his hand.

"You can go home now."

In the hallway passage, he dropped his hat. The Douglas fir floorboards squeaked. Under his weight, all the floors in the house did. He thought he might get around to having them fixed, but he wasn't thinking about that now. Ever since the war had started, he'd been praying for word. Here it was, finally, in his hands. The yard out back was nothing more than sunburnt patches of grass surrounded by a fence missing many of its boards. A shingled shed huddled in the corner, its lock rusted, so that Rain had not bothered to look inside. Someday he would, he'd told himself. Till then he just hoped it wasn't full of anything dead. He sank to the steps and, envelope quivering in his hands, he opened the letter.

Inside the house, Helen, going nowhere, made her way noisily about the kitchen, peering periodically out the window.

HELEN HAD AN APRON ABOUT her waist and was washing the chipped mugs and cutlery in the sink when Rain came inside.

"How quickly can I get to Paris?"

"You mean, France?"

Rain nodded, slowly, still looking at the letter in his hand. "Why?"

"It's Nora."

Helen stared at him, then grabbed the dishtowel hanging by the refrigerator and tried rubbing the glaze off the mugs.

"Never heard you talk of a...Nora. Who's that?"

But Rain couldn't answer.

"Don't get the point of a dessert fork," she said, quickly, angrily, scooping up a handful of wet cutlery. "Why can't they be the same size as a regular one? Piece of cake, piece of steak, all going in the same mouth—"

"Nora needs me, Helen."

She slammed the mismatched forks down on the counter. "Does she know there's a war on?"

He looked up. "She's just a child." *My child.* "Her mother wants me to take her to England."

"I know you think I don't care about what's going on in the world," she said, hastily untying the apron and yanking it free. "But I do. Fine time for you to go over there. Why can't she do it?"

"Lily's husband—he's in the government. They can't leave the country, not now. But Lily's worried about Nora if there's an invasion. If I can get her to England, she can stay with her aunt. And—"

"What?"

"Nora knows me. She'll go with me." *I owe this to her.*

"This...*Lily*," Helen said the name as if she guessed there was a lot more Rain didn't want her to know, "expects you to go all the way to France to take her child out of the country, in the middle of a war?"

"There's still time—"

"That so? I'll just call up Mr. Hitler and ask him what his plans are."

"Helen, please."

She grabbed her hat and handbag and let the door slam behind her.

WHEN HELEN RETURNED SEVERAL HOURS later, she found Rain packing the one bag he owned, the same one he'd arrived with.

"You still goin'?"

"I have to, Helen."

"Then here." She thrust a large brown envelope at him. "I got you on a milk run to Paris. And don't blame me that it cost $700."

Rain pulled the tickets out.

"I went through a helluva lot of trouble to get those, so you'd better come back."

THE MOST DIFFICULT PART OF the entire journey, it now seemed to a weary Rain, was getting a cab in Paris. The city he fondly remembered, with its sweet cinnamon pastries he couldn't afford and chicken-legged chorus girls at Bricktop's on the rue Pigalle, was huddled behind turned-up collars against an icy sleet.

The flights had been long, delayed, and sleepless, his fellow passengers either military officers or company officials anxiously hoping to salvage foreign assets from a war that, so far, was not a war. No one was very talkative and everyone, especially the officers, although trying not to, kept an eye to the sky outside the cabin windows for the spectre of enemy aircraft. Helen had purchased two seats for Rain so that he would be comfortable; however, the extra seat had been commandeered by a loudly snoring captain. The airports were noisy and confusing.

European news was ever more ominous, impossible to ignore. Shortly before Rain left London for Paris, he was able to send Lily a cable: ON MY WAY. STOP.

Finally he found a taxi that agreed to the fare, although the driver made it seem like it was a grave imposition.

Rain's French came back haltingly, along with memories of the wet and stink of the trenches. War to end all war. Laughing boys who, it now appeared, had died entirely in vain. The joke was on them.

As the taxi swerved its way through the crowded Paris suburbs, the driver angrily hollering and waving at anyone who got in his way, Rain pulled out Lily's letter. *I need you.* Not I love you, but close enough. And maybe it didn't matter so much anymore. Because there was Nora. Three years was a lifetime for a child. Would she remember him? Would he still be dear to her? Would she think he'd deserted her? Now, here he was again, back to bounce her away from war on a shoulder ride she was probably too old for.

LILY CLUNG TO HIM FOR a full minute, right there in the hallway. She might have hugged him longer had it not been for Pierre.

"*Mon cher*, let the man breathe."

"Yes. My dear thing, are you very tired? You must excuse us. We've only Madam Racine these days, and she's gone for the evening. Come, let me show you to your room."

Pierre added in that formal French way of his that a light supper would be waiting, perhaps after Rain had bathed and changed his clothes.

When Rain took the stairs he saw her, barely contained at the top, a small beagle by her side. She was taller, but only by a bit. Still, the new inches were years to regret having been absent.

She was indeed too big now for shoulder rides. Pierre was saying something about her staying in her room until she was called. No one listened. Nora's mousy brown hair was cut like a pageboy's. She was thinner, no longer a child. Quite the young lady, Lily said. Nora and Rain tumbled to meet halfway, cheered on by the barking dog, where Nora jumped off a step and into his arms.

NORA CALLED HER DOG HARRY—not Harry she said, but Har-*ri*, and he'd come last summer, so he was still a puppy, with big paws.

"Nora, darling, make your mother happy and eat something."

To Rain, Lily explained that getting food into her over the last few days had been next to impossible. Then she shrugged. Her daughter was excited about his visit.

The girl was sitting beside Rain, her head leaning on his arm. Oh, and that smile. Harry sat expectantly at their feet, waiting for a morsel of food to fall. Nora was very happy Rain had come to take her to London to visit her aunt because now she could practice her English all the time. Monsieur Pierre did not like her speaking English.

"You're not in London yet," said Pierre. He was standing in the doorway of the dining room, pouring himself a drink. Rain felt there was something unusual about the man he couldn't quite articulate. It wasn't until later that night, in bed with space to think, that the realization came. Yes, that was it—everyone in Paris seemed afraid of what was coming. Except Pierre.

"Nora, time for bed, now," he said, returning with his drink. "Your mother and I have to talk with monsieur about the trip. Be a good girl."

Nora squeezed Rain. "You'll be here in the morning? Promise?"

"I promise."

Lily still had to peel the girl off him and, taking her by the hand, lead her and Harry upstairs.

Pierre sat at the table, offered Rain a cigarette, took one himself. "Very kind of you to come all this way."

Rain wanted to say that he'd happily do anything for Lily, but instead he said Nora.

"Your flight?"

"Long. Delayed in London, border-control papers, that sort of thing. I seem to be the only one not involved in the war coming this way."

Rain wondered what Pierre did in his government job and if it involved never believing anything he heard. He certainly looked at Rain that way now.

"Nonetheless, we owe you a great debt. You've put Lily's mind at ease. We could think of no one else we could trust with whom Nora would happily travel."

He poured Rain a drink. "Forgive me for getting to the matter so urgently, but now that you're here, we can make the final arrangements."

"Are things that bad?"

"Hitler has used this time to prepare for an attack, and it will come." Pierre tilted his head and let go a long stream of smoke. "The British are sending much of their remaining embassy staff back to London in a few days. You and the girl will accompany them. An easy trip, you will soon be in England. Lily says the child's aunt has agreed to take her. You'll be back safe in America in a week."

Pierre pushed himself away from the table and rubbed out his cigarette in his plate. "Go and get some sleep."

RAIN REACHED FOR HIS WATCH on the bedside table and knocked it on the floor. The winter sunlight through the curtains was disorienting as he wrapped a blanket about him and stepped onto the landing. Down a few stairs, he could see into the passageway where Pierre had the yelping puppy by its neck and tail and was rubbing its nose back and forth in a puddle of urine, then tossed him outside into the garden and shut the door. To Madame Racine, who watched without expression, and who must have just arrived, for the housekeeper was still in her coat, Pierre said, "*Nettoie ça.*"

"Ah, you are awake." Pierre put on his hat and took his briefcase. "I must get to the ministry early. Lily will see to you."

The door closed behind the man, and Rain, knowing sleep would not come now, sat in the sitting room facing the garden. Winter had emptied the linden and turned the beds brown. Curled leaves whipped about the small dog, who sat shivering on the stone paving. Opening the door, Rain let Harry in, and the dog happily licked his fingers in thanks.

"Monsieur won't care for that," Madame Racine shouted from the kitchen.

RAIN HAD BREAKFAST ALONE, anticipating the day with Nora when he heard Lily on the stairs. Through the door of the dining room he watched her carefully seat the hat on her head. My God, but she was still so beautiful, he thought. Unlike him she hadn't aged a day or put on a pound.

The chair scraped out behind him as Rain stood when she entered the room.

"Madam Racine has prepared you something? Good."

"Where's Nora?"

"Oh, that child of mine has gone and overdone it. I told her this would happen. She was so excited when she heard you were coming that she hasn't slept, and practically not eaten a thing. Now she's gone and got herself ill. A light fever, mind you, and I've told her to stay in bed. Pierre will be angry. He doesn't care for sick children. You don't mind looking in on her, do you? I've got so much to do these days and who knows what shops will still be open."

Then she was gone in an icy blast from the front door.

Rain found Nora in her bed, looking pale and listlessly thumbing through her well-read copy of *Tintin en Amérique*.

"I want to go to the park," she said, but clearly looked without the energy. Harry was curled at her feet with big watchful eyes.

Rain glanced out the window and fibbed about it being cold enough to make their noses fall off, maybe it would even snow. Best they stay put.

"But I love snow."

"How about I read to you and we'll wait for it?"

At midday, Madam Racine brought them lunch on a tray, but Nora did not eat. Rain thought her fever worse and asked the housekeeper what she thought. Madam felt Nora's forehead, then shrugged. What did she know about other women's children?

"She'll be running around with that dog of hers in the morning," said Lily over dinner.

Pierre agreed, the child better be well. The British were leaving for England the day after tomorrow. Rain and Nora would go with them as planned.

But after spending the night wearily vomiting, Nora was clearly worse. Not only did she have a fever, but she now had a bright rash creeping across her chest and reddening her face. Madam Racine was sent to get the doctor. There must be a needle or drops to give the child. She had to be on her way to Calais at dawn.

"This young lady is going nowhere," said the doctor. "Scarlet fever."

"Will she be all right?"

The doctor thanked Rain for handing him his coat. "A few more days of fever, then we shall see."

Rain did not sleep that night, and every hour or so he crept across the landing to quietly open Nora's door. Harry would lift his head, but did not leave Nora's side. Rain had no idea if there was anything he could do to help, other than to make sure she was still breathing. As he moved between his room and the child's, there was no failing to overhear the conversation downstairs.

"I blame you. You indulge that girl."

"I know, Pierre. I'm sorry."

"What are we to do now?"

"She can still go. He'll take care of her."

The crack of an open hand striking her beautiful cheek. Rain gripped the bannister.

"Are you an idiot as well as empty-headed? She's contagious. If I get sick—"

"No, of course, my darling. I'll keep her in her room."

"Damn you, this is not what we agreed."

"Forgive me."

"If there's not some way to get her out of here, then you'd better hope—"

An angry splash of liquid into crystal ended the conversation, and Rain closed the door to his room.

LILY PRESSED THE COMPRESS on her sleeping child's forehead.

"You mustn't think badly of Pierre. He has a very important job. President Lebrun depends on him. Do you know, I've actually had dinner at the Élysée Palace? Can you imagine the look on that silly ol' sister's face at Bon Sauveur if—"

"I heard what he said, Lily."

"Oh, that was nothing. He's under a great deal of stress. The government is evacuating Paris."

"It's come to that?"

"To Bordeaux. That's why Nora must go."

"The government fears an attack that much?"

"Some do. Not Pierre, I think. He's rather fond of what Hitler has done, though I don't think the President knows that."

"Come with us."

Lily looked about nervously, as if she'd lost her place on a stage and needed a cue. "Where?"

"London. Andrew's sister will take you both in, surely."

"And *I'm* sure as far as she's concerned I was the ruin of her brother."

"She agreed to take Nora. That's something."

Lily wrung out the compress in the dish of cool water by Nora's bed.

"Lily, Evie does know we're coming? Lily? Oh, Jesus."

"You see how Pierre is with her. I had to do something."

"I see how he treats you."

"If not for Pierre, we'd be beggars. I will not have my child go hungry in the street. Not like—"

She had been.

"You don't have to stay with him. Come with me to California, both of you."

"What? To America?"

"Why not? She's my child too, so you say."

Lily slowly shook her head as she gently pulled away the curls from Nora's sleeping face. Harry's watchful eyes kept their vigil.

"Then let her come with me. If the war gets to Britain, she'll be safer."

"And how would I explain that to Pierre, huh? He thinks you're an old acquaintance, nothing more. Besides, it might not even come to that. Pierre says any war will be over in six months. No one can beat the Nazis. Just get her to London. She'll be safe there until I can figure out what to do. Evie won't turn you away if she believes Nora is Andrew's, and he's dead. How could she know otherwise?" She glanced up defiantly. "I'm not the best of mothers, but even I couldn't bear to have an ocean between us."

MADAME RACINE'S HUSBAND knew the green grocer, Laurent, whose son Roland was in the army, and it was Roland who said in March that the Germans were massing on the other side of the Maginot Line.

"Pierre says the fortification will hold them."

Rain was not as confident as Lily. He'd been in Paris for over a month now and was anxious to leave. The newsreels back in September had shown how the Germans flew right over border defenses in Poland. Did Lily really need to go to Bordeaux right now?

"I've no choice. Pierre called to say he found a flat. A rather nice one, I should think, on the rue de Mulet."

"What about Nora?"

"You heard the doctor. He says her rash is better. She'll be running around with that dog of hers in no time, and she has you to watch out for her. If anything goes wrong, you know how to get word to me."

"I'm not so sure."

"Darling, this is what I do. Pierre has to go because the government is moving and he needs me to make the apartment ready. You can only imagine what condition it's in, from *those* people who used to live there. Pierre's been assigned to Marshal Pétain and he's expected to entertain ministers, ambassadors, even generals in the army. I'll have days of shopping ahead to get the place right. And a cook. Where will I find a cook under these conditions?"

"Parties? With the Germans coming?"

"You know what I mean."

Madam Racine carried the last of the suitcases down the stairs to the front door, where the driver took them and placed them in the waiting taxi. Lily checked herself in the mirror one last time. She seemed pleased with what she saw. Rain not so much anymore.

Lily caught him watching.

"It won't be for long. As soon as Pierre has another way for you and Nora to get to England, we'll be back."

THE DOCTOR CONFESSED HE WAS worried about Nora's progress. With the redness on her skin beginning to fade after a week, she should be more active by now.

"The light hurts," Nora complained, even when her drapes were shut, and the weakest broth, slowly spoon-fed, still refused to stay down. After her neck became so sore that she could barely move without screaming, the doctor realized his worst fears.

"Meningitis."

"Is that bad?"

"Her mother must come home."

Rain looked at the girl, so tiny she appeared to be swallowed up by her bed. Harry alert and ready to jump in after her.

"I'm supposed to take her to England."

The doctor repacked his case then took Rain's arm as if to underscore the need to understand. "This child will not be leaving her bed for weeks, if she leaves it at all."

"It can't be that bad?"

"Like I said, her mother must come home."

LILY'S VOICE ON THE TELEPHONE was distant and tearful. She loved Nora, she adored Nora, Nora was her life, but she just couldn't take the train to Paris right now. Everything was such a muddle. Pierre needed her. If Rain only knew how much there was to do; why, Lily hardly slept at all—and the lists? She was sure she was making lists in her sleep, of all the dishes, linens, and alterations the apartment needed and with the war, and rations, and uncertainty, well, goodness, she wasn't a magician. Would Rain be her dearest friend in the world for just a bit longer, and stay with Nora? "And not to worry, Pierre's arranging passage across the Channel."

Rain put down the receiver and looked into Harry's big eyes. The dog had taken to following him around the house when Nora slept.

"*Pas apte à être une mère à un chat,*" Madam Racine said from the kitchen with a snort, almost as if it were a nursery rhyme, having guessed Lily's response.

The telegram from Helen, all words in uppercase, sounded angry. Mrs. Vroman didn't care to have her garden sitting area waiting all this time to be finished. What about the other jobs he'd lined up? Did Rain have any idea when he'd be returning?

NO. STOP.

As Nora worsened, Rain slept in a chair near her bed.

"Monsieur, you don't look well. You must take care of your own health or you will be of no use," the doctor cautioned on his last visit.

The army had come for him; there was nothing more he could do for the child. He wished Rain well and hoped he'd get Nora safely out of Paris. An invasion, he shook his head sadly, must be weeks, maybe even days away.

When he could, Rain took Harry out on the empty, wet streets under dull skies. Even the sun was evacuating. He raked the garden, hoping that one day he'd bring Nora back down onto the grass, wondering if she'd ever see it again, then circled about and pounded fists—*stupid stupid stupid*—for even imagining such a thing.

He cried. Just like that. On his knees, hands full of weeds as he sought to unclog the bed for unfolding narcissi. Nora couldn't die, she just couldn't. For all Lily's protestations, he knew Nora meant little to her mother. He and Nora: both Lily's darling things. Lily might recover from the loss, but not Rain. *Damn it. Damn her.* The old gardener at Bon Sauveur had been right about ivy. Rain should have uprooted her from his life years ago. Chance after chance and here he was, back in France, another war. Endless circles of Lily. But now Nora was entangled just as much as he was.

He began the garden in Nora's room that very day. Rain moved her desk and bookcase away from the wall and sketched out the flowers. A rose, a cornflower, a lily, and a crane flower, oversized and almost to the ceiling, their leaves intertwined as they kicked up their stems in a cancan.

"Monsieur Pierre won't care for that," Madame Racine said from the hallway, bringing a tray. But she smiled and looked in often on the progress.

Using the tubes of gouache from Nora's desk, Rain gave the flowers thick red lips and long blue lashes over laughing eyes. The rose he made pink, the cornflower, dark blue. The lily was orange with purple specks and the spiked crane flower petals bright yellow. He gave them all red satin dresses with frothy white crinolines peeking out from underneath.

"Which is your favourite?" he asked, when he caught Nora smiling.

"The blue one."

"Mine too."

Every day the girl slept less, ate a bit more, sat up, and even petted Harry.

"You know, I once made a garden like this for your mother, out of chalk, as a Christmas present."

"Did she like it?"

"Oh, yes. She said it was the best present she ever got, until she got you."

MADAM RACINE ARRIVED FOR WORK that morning at the end of April, loudly, as was her custom, but she didn't remove her coat or hat. Rain was already in the kitchen boiling water for tea.

"Oh, monsieur, I am so sorry to have to say this, but I give notice."

Rain found it hard to make out her words through all the tears and the handkerchief that kept getting placed over her mouth.

"My husband says we must leave Paris. We are going south today, to Lourdes. My brother-in-law has a farm nearby. We shall be safe there. Even that Hitler would not dare to invade the city of Our Lady and Saint Bernadette."

Madam Racine crossed herself, her last words angry and therefore regrettably sinful.

Not to worry, she'd not leave them to starve. A pot of soup was on the stove and there were several loaves of bread—but monsieur must not put off calling the child's mother. If they were ever going to get to England, they must go now. Today. The grocer's son, Roland, had been sent with troops to the border.

🝆🝆🝆

"I LIKE BEING HERE with just you," said Nora, swinging her legs at the kitchen table.

"What about Harry?"

"Oh, yes. Him to."

She was nibbling a piece of bread that Rain feared he'd cut too thick, put too much butter on. He fished bits of chicken out of the soup pot for the dog.

With May came the sun, finally, and warmer weather. Rain got Nora out of bed each day and they spent a few hours in the garden. Harry rolled on the grass and chased his ball into the spikey veronica. Nora slowly got the strength back in her legs and danced, only a little, to be sure she hadn't forgotten any of her ballet lessons. Rain thought about tanks.

After Madam Racine left, news was harder to come by. Rain didn't like to leave Nora even to buy a newspaper, if any were still printing. The grocer around the corner had closed and boarded up his shop. The rue de Fleurus was quiet at times of the day when it had no right to be. Lily telephoned to say that she'd been trying to get through for ages but the lines were busy and that Pierre had found a way to get Rain and Nora to Calais, but travel from Bordeaux, travel anywhere in France if you weren't in the army, was difficult. The last telegram from Helen begged him to come home. He could almost hear her tears.

"Hey, I got a great idea. Why don't we live here?" asked Nora, seeing the suitcases with no place to go.

"What about your auntie? Don't you want to visit her?"

Nora shrugged. "I've never seen her."

"She'll be very happy to meet you."

"Will I have my own room?"

"*Mais oui.*"

"A big one?"

"Enough room for you and Harry and maybe a small elephant."

"Can you stay, too?"

"I'm bigger than a small elephant, and I must get home. You'll want to spend time with your aunt Evie."

Harry dropped the ball at Nora's feet.

"Is she nice?"

"How can she not be? She is your aunt, and you'll love visiting her in London. Maybe she'll take you to the zoo. They have a real elephant."

"But I want to go to the zoo with you."

Rain smiled.

"Will mama and Monsieur Pierre be coming to London?"

"No, Monsieur Pierre has very important work to do with the army."

Nora sighed a big grown-up sigh as she rolled the ball on the grass for Harry. "Monsieur Pierre is always cross. He makes mama sad."

THE WOMAN WAS SOBBING, tearful, and her words, when she could get them out, were a kind of wail. She was far away and what she said, kept saying, about Belgium took time to float through Rain's open window. He'd not slept well; the hot night, and a few glasses of wine, maybe more, had not helped. Now, as he lay against damp sheets and listened to the distant cries of the woman making their way over the Paris rooftops, the world seeped in.

The invasion had begun.

Rain sat up.

*Damn Lily.* No word in days, no telegram, no telephone call, and now the Germans were coming. What was he going to do? He couldn't be trapped in France, not again. He got up and went to the window. If only the streets outside would erupt into chaos and panic and not this bloody quiet. How could there be a war on with empty streets and no one but Rain caring? Even the wailing woman had stopped.

He couldn't show his fear to Nora.

*Right.*

Much to do. A telegram to Helen, saying what, he didn't know. Money? How much money could he get his hands on? He'd try again to get word to Lily but if he couldn't, was he prepared to take Nora and head for what—the coast? She seemed well enough now to make the trip. They could be in London in a couple of days. Food? He should see about food. There'd be a run for what was left in the shops and markets and he'd have to make sure he had enough to get them to Calais. But how would they get there? Train? Hired car?

Harry's nails clicked across the wooden floor outside his room, followed by Nora's bare feet.

*Damn you, Lily.*


As Nora took a pencil and practiced writing her own telegram, *Please Mr. Hitler do not come to France,* Rain cabled Helen to say he was finally leaving Paris for London.

"But monsieur," the operator explained, a fellow with an unstarched collar and circles under his eyes, "there's no way of knowing when the message can be sent." The government had taken over all communications. The line of people behind Rain stretched out onto the boulevard.

Surely the man must have some idea.

"No, no."

Wherever Rain went, the same thing. When is the next train? Could he buy a ticket? Were they still running north?

"Try again in the morning."

After supper, Nora sat on her bed and contemplated what must come. Her white suitcase looked so big when it was empty but seemed to fill up with only one doll.

Maybe only clothes, suggested Rain.

"Yes, they're better here," she agreed, meaning she was now too old for toys.

Rain dabbled at the garden on her wall to occupy his mind, giving the dancing flowers blocky wooden shoes, one of which the rose managed to kick across the ceiling. The delicate painting, Nora's chatter, and the sound of Harry chewing a stocking filled with an old towel, helped Rain to keep his hands steady, not think too much about how the countryside had changed in twenty years or whether he could find his way to the coast on his own. A map, where could he get a map? How much longer did he dare wait to hear from Lily? If the Germans reached Paris—

Yes, if the Germans reached Paris.

LILY AND PIERRE RETURNED FROM Bordeaux two days later, tired, put out. Nothing in the country was running on time. But Lily was wrapped in shimmering blue Russian sable, a coat much too warm for the May day. She held it about her as if it were too big, as if it had belonged to a larger woman.

"You've no idea what we've been through. Everything is so uncertain. We were going to have to sit on a train for three days until Pierre requisitioned a car and driver and said we just had to be back in Paris. Where's Madam Racine? She will have to see to dinner."

Rain explained that she and her husband were hiding with the Virgin in Lourdes.

"Really? How inconvenient."

"*Mon Dieu*, woman, for once, find your way around the kitchen."

Pierre wanted to talk to Rain.

In his office, he poured them a drink, then closed out the sound of Nora and her mother banging pots, Nora singing, Lily whining.

"Forgive her, monsieur. That woman can be a child at times, but maybe that will see her through whatever is coming."

Forgive Lily? Rain had known her since she was a girl, had loved her every day since. He had earned the right to hate her. How dare this man make apologies for her now.

"Between you and I, France cannot defend herself for long, if at all." Pierre drained his glass, refilled it, and tapped Rain on the shoulder. "But you must not worry. You and the child leave in the morning. By this time tomorrow evening, you shall be safely crossing the Channel."

"Does Nora know?"

"Let's leave that to her mother. Give them one more night thinking their merry world goes on."

MONSIEUR AND MADAM ROBILLARD arrived early the next morning in a blue Citroën that sometimes coughed and whose front, Nora exclaimed, had a wide silver mouth with a round eye on each side.

"Don't be fooled by the stooped shoulders and grey hair," Pierre said confidentially to Rain in the hallway. The couple had spent the last war as agents for the Belgian government. He slipped Rain a handful of notes. "Not much. A thousand francs, a few pounds. It's all I could get my hands on. In case you need it."

Lily came down the stairs with Nora, looking happy, but Rain could tell from the swollen and red eyes how she'd spent the night.

"Now, my darling, you must listen to everything monsieur says."

Nora nodded, but maybe going in the car and leaving her mother wasn't such a great idea after all, now that the time had come.

"It's only for a few days, and look, the sun is here. What a wonderful morning for a drive to the coast. As soon as I can, I shall come to London too."

"Promise, Mama?"

Lily hugged her daughter, and by the strength of her embrace, threatened to reveal there was indeed something to fear.

Monsieur Robillard held open the Citroën's back door. "Mademoiselle, your carriage awaits."

Nora informed him that it wasn't a carriage because it didn't have a horse attached to the front.

"Mademoiselle Nora, you and I are going to be great friends. I know it."

Rain, left alone on the walk in front of the house, nodded to both Pierre and Lily. He had no right to anything else. "I'll get her safely to London."

"Wait!"

Lily ran down the steps and into his arms.

"Now Lily, they must be off," Pierre scolded.

From behind him, Harry scraped and yelped at the closed door.

"I shall never forget this."

*I love you*, is what Rain heard.

He bent his mouth to her ear. "Change your mind. Come with us." *Come with me.*

Lily pulled back and wiped her eyes. "You know I won't." She kissed his cheek. "Here."

She handed him an envelope. "It's a letter to Evie. You'll find her address in there. I did write to her from Bordeaux, really this time, but who can say with the mail these days."

"And if she doesn't take Nora?"

"She will. For once, I'm glad she cares more about her family's reputation." She took Rain's arm and walked him the few paces to the car. "Let's not make this goodbye."

"Mama, Harry!"

"Oh, Nora, I think it best if he stays here with us."

"No! I can't leave Harry!"

The delicately negotiated truce over the gorge of separation threatened to collapse. There'd be no getting Nora to Calais should that happen.

"Let the dog come," said Rain.


THE STREETS WERE CLOGGED with automobiles, trucks, moving vans with chairs and mattresses tied to the roof, horse-pulled wagons and throngs of people carrying suitcases all on the way to Calais, it seemed to Rain. *How will so many of us get across the Channel?*

Monsieur Robillard, seventy if a day thought Rain, eased the Citroën through the crawling traffic and, if compelled to swear at someone cutting in front of him, did so quietly and with such grace that Nora never knew.

"After we are free of the city," he said, "smooth sailing all the way."

Around noon, Madam Robillard pulled a wooden box covered in leather and tied shut with twine from under her feet and passed around bread and cheese.

"We make the cheese at our farm," she said. "And here, tea." In a flask. English tea.

But the roads outside of Paris were just as congested, perhaps even worse, for army convoys had to pass and everyone was ordered off to the side. By evening, they'd only made it as far as Amiens.

"Find some quiet place to stop," Madam Robillard told her husband. She glanced in the back seat at Nora. "We'll sleep in the car, little one. Won't that be an adventure? I bet you've never slept in a car before."

Nora shook her head.

"We have lots to eat, and blankets. In the morning, we'll be on our way. And early, old man. We get to Calais by midday."

But if anything, the roads north from the city the next morning were worse than anything they'd experienced since leaving Paris.

"People stopping to listen to gossip. If they'd get on with their business, we'd all be on our way," said madam.

Rain asked what she'd heard from the cyclists who'd been riding alongside the car.

"The Germans have Belgium," she said quietly. "That, we knew would happen."

"Are they in France?"

"Let's hope not."

After a lunch of bread and strawberry jam, Madam Robillard told her husband she'd had enough of the crawling. Go east, she told him. The back roads would get them north faster because everyone would be afraid to be so near what could be the front.

But would it be safe, Rain asked when they stopped to let Nora take Harry to water the grass.

"What? An old couple out for a drive with a child? And you, monsieur, you must excuse me, but you hardly look like a spy. Your French is good. Don't speak English anymore."

Rain was not put at ease. He and Nora were supposed to be in London by now, yet here they were, closer than ever to the advancing Germans. Madam Robillard was correct, however, in that the roads were less clogged, and as her husband kept veering to the northeast, they became almost empty.

"No one will miss this," she said, handing a piece of cheese to Nora. "*Pour le chien.*"

They passed a man and woman with suitcases bouncing against the sides of their knees, a line of children behind them. Madame told her husband they should stop at the clump of trees up ahead for the night.

"Can't be helped, monsieur. One more night in the car but tomorrow, absolutely, you and the girl will be in Calais."

Rain held his tongue and his fear. The old couple was only trying to help. After he and Nora were safe at the coast, then what would they do?

"We go back to Paris and wait this out. What does a war want with the likes of us?"

Parked under the trees, Rain watched Nora lead Harry into the farmer's fields, though he wasn't sure who was doing the chasing. The walking family reached the parked car. The oldest of the children was a boy, maybe seventeen, sullen and looking back towards Paris. Rain remembered that foolish age all too well, how easy jingles and posters about honour and duty could turn a boy into fodder. The youngest child looked to be about Nora's age. Monsieur Robillard waved them a safe journey after his wife handed over some of her extra apples.

Monsieur Robillard took off his hat and rubbed the back of his head. "The man says he heard the Germans are outside Calais, and will soon cut off Boulogne."

"But that's where we're going."

"You can't take every rumour as true. In the morning, we get closer. If we have to, maybe we go west, or we go south."

"What? Back to Paris?"

"No, no. To Dieppe. Longer yes, but we can get a boat from there."

But not anytime soon. Rain leaned against the car and closed his eyes. If only he could open them and be in London and not in some French field watching Nora chasing Harry, running towards him, pointing at the sky.

"*Les avions!*"

Rain saw nothing, heard nothing.

"What is it?" madam asked, shielding her eyes from the glare. "Airplanes?"

"Yes, there!" Nora pointed to just over the horizon.

In the setting sun, Rain could now see their glint in the sky. The sound of their engines came shortly after. Just up the road, the walking family heard them too and stopped.

Madam Robillard gently squeezed Rain's arm. In her hand was a gun. Very quietly, so as not to frighten the child, she told him to get Nora into the car.

The roaring planes now ripped across the sky and began their descent. Madam Robillard shouted *Aller!* as the ground around Rain hissed, *poof poof poof,* penetrated by the bullets. Nora froze in front of him as he dove at her and pulled her down into the ditch along the road, gathering a mouth full of dirt as he rolled. Holding her head under his chest, he looked up to see the elderly couple as bullets tore through their jerking bodies and shot with tinny *plinks* into the automobile. On the road, the family was running under the low-flying aircraft, which quickly doubled back and let loose another barrage of bullets. Rain held Nora tight, as if squeezing her could shield her from the horror. When he felt something warm and wet on his leg, he thought blood, then was relieved to see that she had only soiled herself.

The planes veering off, Rain ran with Nora in his arms to the other side of the smoking car so that she would not see the old couple, sprawled open-eyed in the grass. He sat her on the seat and reached for her suitcase.

"Let's get you something dry."

Nora was hiccoughing as she slipped a finger into the bullet hole in the upholstery.

"Are they hurt?'

Rain held up a dress and clean underclothes. He took off Nora's shoes and stockings. He glanced up to look for more planes and caught sight of the old woman's leg on the other side of the car.

"No, no, they're sleeping."

The girl wasn't a child, she wouldn't believe him, but she looked like she wanted to. "Where's Harry?"

The dog? No, not the dog too. Hopefully he'd only been scared off by the attack. *Christ in hell.* Every minute as a target under these deadly skies was more anxious than the one before. They needed to be on their way. But to where? Then a small mercy. With Nora calling for him, Harry came running back. Rain leashed the dog to his waist with the twine from the leather food case.

"We have to go."

No more delays.

"But what about Monsieur and Madame Robillard?"

"We'll tell the police what happened."

Rain, not knowing where they would go or what they would encounter, took only what he could carry, mostly food and a coat for Nora. He took her hand, crossed over the ditch, and climbed into the farmer's field, away from the road and the Citroën, with its doors left open, away from the Robillards, and from the bodies of the bullet-ridden children and their parents, all lying in a row.

Rain tried to think. Should they go back to Paris? It was too far, and to what? Lily and Pierre would have evacuated to the southern coast with the last of the French government.

The Germans were close now, perhaps even in Calais. *Jesus.* If only Nora hadn't got sick, she'd be safe in London and he'd back in California. Listening to Helen say she'd have given those Nazis the what-for. *Helen. Calming, blessed Helen!* He'd hug her to pieces if he ever saw her again.

They'd have to walk to the coast. Rain had money. Surely he could find some fisherman to take them across the Channel. He'd row a leaky boat across a river in hell if it came to that, but at least it was a plan. He'd stay in the fields, close to the road, so he'd have a sense of where he was going. Anything was better than waiting for the planes.


RAIN STAGGERED ON IN THE DARK until he could no longer make out what was in front of him. He was glad Nora slept in his arms, and that she did not wake when he sank to his knees, groaned, and placed her amongst the wind-tossed lavender. His legs ached. Without knowing how far they'd come, or how far they had to go, or even where they were, he agonized over how'd they manage come dawn. The girl would be hungry. She'd be afraid and want her mother. And he felt fairly certain he'd not be able to stand. What could he do?

"Here, Harry, lie down."

The weary dog curled up in the space between them, and licked Rain's hand.

Nora stirred. "Are monsieur and madam dead?" Her question, and its sincerity, would not take a lie.

He breathed deeply. Then spoke. "Yes."

So much of Nora's childhood he'd missed. What remained for the both of them had bled out, back there, into the French countryside.

"Will they be okay under the trees?" Nora asked drowsily, as if from a dream.

He stroked her hair, urging her with his touch to rest. "God has already taken them to heaven. Go to sleep. Big day tomorrow."

"Is it all right if I cry a little bit for them?"

"We both will."

"I don't think I can sleep out here," she said. "I've never slept outside."

"Then we must think of a place that makes us happy, and if we pretend really hard, maybe we can go there in our dreams."

"Really? Where will you go?"

The alacrity surprised him. "My kitchen, in America, with my friend Helen. She's always breaking my cups and getting angry with forks. You would like her very much. She makes a good cup of tea."

Nora yawned. "I like how it smells here."

She was asleep before she could share her dream place.

Rain leaned back and stared at the dark sky. Not a single star. If only he could close his eyes. The wind through the lavender hissed about them, tall and waving. Lavender with the briny kiss of the sea. How many hours had it been since they'd eaten? He was too tired to eat now. Save it for Nora. No telling how long until they could find more, or what lay ahead on the road.

"This war's different, Harry," he said.

The dog raised his head and looked at him.

Soldiers killing children on a country road. Civilians, yet they'd not been spared. Nora could just as easily have been shot as the elderly couple back there—

*Stop.*

Rubbing his eyes did not erase the image of their final moments. Harry growled hard in the back of his throat.

Rain saw them too. Lights. A truck on the road.

The dog barked and Rain lunged, grabbed hold, and covered his mouth. The truck slowed down. Had they heard? *Christ.* Now they shone lights into the fields, back and forth. Harry struggled against the twine securing him to Rain's waist. *Shut up, damn you.* The old couple, those children—these soldiers killed for sport. *Harry, be still, please be still.* The truck passed closer, slower. Rain ducked, the dog now in his arms, struggling, determined to sound the alarm, wanting to raise his sleeping mistress.

*Dear God please shut him up.*

The dog's neck was soft and small. The thin leather collar, the silver plate engraved with his name. Rain's hand went easily about its throat.

*They mustn't know we're here.*

Soldiers, their rifles pointed at the fields of lavender, lights waving back and forth.

*Shut up shut up shut up.*

Harry flopped around in his hands, his small teeth tearing at his skin, looking up at him as if to say *I cannot stop. Do it. It's for her. Do it!* Close, so close, until the only movement was the passing tires crackling on the gravel road and Rain could hear the soldiers talking.

French. They were French.

He lay the lifeless dog down, covered his mouth with both hands, and tried to shove his sobbing back down his throat.

IN THE MORNING, RAIN GROANED as he rose to his muscles revolting. There'd been no sleep for him. He'd not be able to carry Nora today if they expected to make any distance. Beside him,

curled in the waving lavender, Nora stared up at the billowing
white clouds with the tint of ash. Rain could only wonder as
to her dreams.

"The air smells funny," she said.

Burning oil, the stench of war, Rain remembered it well.

Breakfast was a crust with the last bit of madame's jam. The
bottle of milk had gone sour.

"Where's Harry?"

"He must have wondered off during the night, chasing a
mouse. He won't be far."

"We can't leave him."

Rain got up stiffly. "He'll find us. Dogs have excellent noses."

"How come we have to walk through fields?"

"Don't you like the lavender? It'll smell very pretty when
all the fields bloom, no?"

Nora trailed Rain, one hand clutching her crust of bread, the
other hand slapping nodding stalks of new blossoms.

"How come so much of it?"

"Farmers grow it for soap and perfume, but over there, I
think there's a field of sunflowers."

After several more miles, Rain realized that the piece of twine
was still tied about his waist. He took it off and was about to toss
it when Nora said no. He'd need it again when Harry found them.

"Remember that song we used to sing? *Quack, quack, quack.*
Come, sing it with me."

But Nora did not sing, nor did the crust of now hard bread
in her hand get eaten.

They curled up for another night under a grove of apple trees
that had gone wild in tall grass. The fruit was meagre and mostly
worm-eaten, but at least enough to stop the rumble of hunger.

In the morning Rain could smell the sea, feel it cool on his
face. Nora needed a proper rest and decent food. Rain decided

the road was worth the risk. They'd seen no one, the skies were clear. Even the smell of smoke was gone. At the next farm, he'd ask, beg for a bed and food.

The house in the distance did not appear until late afternoon. None too soon. The shock of the attack having worn off the child, Nora complained. She'd not go one step further without her dog, couldn't she have something to eat, and why did she have to relieve herself in the grass with nothing to clean up?

The farmhouse was white, with a pitched roof, and a chimney at each end. A barn sat behind with its door wide open. Sheets snapped on lines stretched to a pole. Surely someone was home even if there was no smoke, but when Rain knocked, no answer.

"You said we could stay here."

The whine in Nora's voice made it clear that she'd not walk another step. Rain tried the doorknob.

*"Bonjour?"*

No reply. The fireplaces were cold. In one of the upstairs bedrooms, they found an open suitcase by an empty armoire.

"Where is everyone?"

"Gone away on an adventure, just like us."

Rain sat Nora at the table in the kitchen. Perhaps he could find something to eat.

"Can we stay?"

Tonight they'd rest. If the owners came home, well, god dammit, there was a bloody war on.

WHY COULDN'T THEY LIVE HERE, Nora wanted to know. The house was warm now that the fire was lit, and Harry would love the barn. Mama and Monsieur Pierre could even come.

"Your aunt's waiting for you, remember?"

"Oh, yes. It's very good."

She meant the soup that Rain had stewed with some potatoes and parsnips he'd found once he'd made a fire in the kitchen hearth. Rain was so hungry he would have eaten the arse-end of a dead robin and thought it divine. He'd also found some bread and cheese left in a wooden box by the water pump, several bottles of wine in the kitchen cupboard, and even some eggs in the barn. He drank half a bottle as he prepared the food, before the girl could see. They'd both sleep well tonight, in beds with sheets and pillows, and in the morning, Rain would leave a note and some francs for the owners.

"Take another bite of that cheese," Rain said before he stepped out back for more firewood against the evening chill.

The sun was lowering as he walked back to the house; he'd have to search for candles or a lantern. He could see Nora through the open door, sitting at the table. The two of them together like this, in spite of the reason, it felt good. If only he could hold onto the moment. Maybe it was worth trying to talk Evie into letting him take Nora to America. Maybe he wouldn't have to persuade her at all. Showing up unexpectedly on her doorstep may come with a responsibility she had no intention of shouldering. He would. Gladly. Given the chance, in California, he would create the most perfect garden for Nora, where every season was a joy, and aircraft did not rain death from above. Even Helen would like her eventually, he was sure of it. He banished the thought. He couldn't think that far ahead. She was safe and fed and soon off to bed. For now, that was enough. As he got closer he noticed how still she was sitting, almost motionless, and how she stared at something out of his sight with an expression of terror. The firewood fell to his feet as he ran to the house.

"Nora? Nora!"

She didn't turn to look at him even as he re-entered the kitchen.

In the front doorway stood a young man, his cheeks covered with downy whiskers, his coat rolled under one arm. His other hand was pointing a pistol.

"You speak English?" the stranger said.

Rain nodded.

"Who else is here?"

"No one."

The man shook the gun. "You lie!"

Rain saw it in him, remembered it: the fear. A boy much too young for war.

"Is that wine? Hand it to me."

Rain did so, carefully.

The young man drank deep and fast, red spilling over his cheeks as he kept the shaking gun pointed at them.

"You got food?"

"Soup. Eggs, too."

The man reached across the table and grabbed the loaf of bread.

"How long since you ate?"

"Couple o' days, maybe. I'll take some of that soup."

Rain filled a bowl. The man sat down and dropped his rolled jacket.

"Could you put the gun away? You're frightening the child."

"And you, big man? Do I frighten you?"

"I'm too afraid of the Germans to worry about one British corporal." He nodded at the chevron on the man's jacket.

"Fucking hell." Then to Nora, "Apologies, little lady."

Some of the wildness about the lanky corporal dissipated as he ate, and he tucked the pistol into his belt.

"You're no Frenchy, mate."

"We're trying to get to England. We were on our way to Calais when we were attacked."

"Calais?" The corporal drank again and wiped his mouth with his hand. "Jerries got the whole bloody place. Sent us off swimming like rats in the Channel. Probably toasting Herr Hitler in Paris right now."

"What about the army?"

"Hands up without a whimper." The corporal pounded the table and Nora clutched at Rain. "Fucking French."

Rain swallowed. "The Germans are in Calais?"

"You got shite in your ears, mate? Boulogne too. They got the whole fucking northern coast. Everyone. Except me."

THE CORPORAL MADE Rain and Nora sleep in the front room where he could keep an eye on them. He had a hair trigger for a finger, he cautioned, so Rain better not try anything. He clutched another bottle of wine. Rain poked the fire, added more logs, then sat by Nora who lay on the sofa.

"You get that in the last war?" the corporal asked, meaning Rain's face.

Rain nodded.

The corporal drank, handed over the bottle.

"How many of your men did you lose?" asked Rain.

"Too many."

Rain nodded. "Don't blame yourself."

"What the fuck would you know?"

"Enough that you've got to live with what's left."

"Yeah, well, tell that to their wives and kids."

"How did it happen?"

"I said *shut up*, will ya?"

Rain watched the young man stare down the flames. "I outlived a whole regiment," he said. "For a long time, I wondered why. Why did someone like me live and so many others die that day."

The soldier took another swig, failing at looking cocky. "Yeah? What's the answer?"

Rain gently rubbed Nora's arm. "Until now, I never had one."

The corporal would not be able to fight sleep much longer. "So, what are you? Some kind of saint?"

Nora stirred. Her dreams were not pleasant.

"How are you getting back to England—"

"Jesus, man, haven't you heard a word I've said? There's no...getting...back...."

After the corporal began to snore, Rain carefully pulled the gun from the young man's belt. He placed it on the table beside him. He did not want the corporal rolling over during the night and shooting himself.

NORA PUT DOWN HER FORK when the young man appeared at breakfast.

He rubbed his head, looking at the gun in his other hand, as if he were perplexed, or hungover, or possibly both.

"Why didn't you take it?"

Rain pointed to the bowl of eggs and the pot of tea. "I figured a soldier needs it more than we do."

They ate in silence. When the corporal had finished his strong cup of tea, he sat back and asked, "So, what now?"

Rain eyed him. "Keep walking for the coast. Hopefully find a boat or someone to take us across."

The young man shook his head. "You're crazy, mate, you know that? Even if you do manage to find someone, the Jerries got U-boats in the Channel."

"What's a U-boat?" Nora wanted to know.

Rain served her the last spoonful of eggs. "Special boats that go underwater to make sure you're safe."

"Okay, I get it," said the corporal. "You're still determined to go?"

"I promised her mother I'd get her safely to England."

"Goddammit. All right then. I figure we're about four, five miles to the coast. I can at least get you that far. After that, God help ya."

"IS HE COMING BACK?"

Rain wasn't so sure, but nodded anyway.

"He's like Roland, at the grocer's," said Nora. "He's just a boy too."

Below them, grass bent low in the chilly hard wind and clung to the bluff, all broken and sandy, stones tumbling and crumbling down to the beach and the white tips of the English Channel. Rain wrapped his coat around Nora. The long day of walking ended here. There was nowhere else to go. The sun set and the sky lay in layers from orange, to pink, and now blue.

*You got any money?* the corporal had asked.

*What for?*

*Come this far, damn foolish not to make a dash for it.*

Rain had handed over almost everything he had. Now he wished he hadn't. Part of him knew they'd never see the young man again. It saddened him for Nora's sake. What would he do now? The Germans behind them, the sea ahead. If it were just Rain, he'd walk down to the beach and keep on going. How long would it take a man to drown, he wondered—

"Harry's not coming, is he?"

"I think he's happier here."

"Is he dead like madame and monsieur?"

Rain stared at the waves rolling in one after the other after the other, his hand rubbing the tightness in his chest.

"I'm glad," Nora said. "Harry's a French dog. He wouldn't understand anything Auntie says."

IN THE HOUR BEFORE DAWN the corporal returned, crawling noisily up the steep embankment where he'd left Rain and Nora.

"Wakey, wakey, mate. Let's go. And don't look so surprised. Makes me think you thought the worse o' me."

"What? Where?"

He pointed to the beach and the sad little rowboat, *L'Acadie*, almost faded from the transom. "Seen better days, and don't for Christ's sake ask me what I had to do to get my hands on 'er. You okay?"

Rain could only manage a nod.

"Come on."


RAIN TOOK HIS TURN AFTER the corporal and rowed until his hands blistered, then bled, and every pull of the oars was accompanied by a long, silent scream. He didn't want the corporal to think he wasn't up to his share, but truly, he wasn't. Little food, little sleep—how long now? He couldn't even recall.

They rowed against the chop in the searing sun, high winds, whitening caps, each wave closer to freedom, but not yet. How many hours? How many miles? Thirty, maybe forty, said the corporal. If only the soldier hadn't said anything about the submarines. They had no food, no water, and poor, frightened Nora, whose job was to bail with the biscuit tin they'd found on the beach and keep an eye out for England, saw nothing except gulls and seaweed—and the fishing boat coming towards them.

Rain nudged the corporal awake with his foot.

"Christ."

"What do you think?"

"I hope to hell she's British."

The boat made for them, pulled alongside. Its deck full of grim-faced, huddling soldiers pulled from French beaches.

Rain found himself weeping, so that Nora, afraid, clung to him and wondered if he was okay. Were they going home now?

"Thank God."

The corporal was less emotional. "Looks like I got passage back to the war."

RAIN CARRIED HIS SLEEPING NORA from the station. His empty pockets meant no money for a cab, not that he could see one that was not already commandeered by the army. He would have to try and cable Helen for funds to get him home, but for now he'd throw himself on the generosity of Andrew's sister.

On the Belgrave Mews, he awkwardly fished out Lily's letter to check the address. Up ahead. At last. He stopped at the narrow townhouse, with white-painted brick and black iron grills over the windows.

"Never expected to see *you* again," Evie said. She was older, greyer, pulling the sleeping child from Rain's bone-weary arms. "You took your time getting here."

"You got Lily's letter?"

"Yes, I got it. Barely legible. Woman writes like a child."

Rain made to follow her inside.

"Where do you think you're going?"

"I thought—"

"No doubt you did. That woman squandered my brother's fortune, and his life, and now expects me, with no means, to care for my brother's child I knew nothing about until a few days ago."

"I'm sorry, I'm sure—"

"Good day."

"Wait! I can take her. I want to. To America. Just give me a few days to arrange it."

The woman did not look kindly on Rain's hand on her door.

"You? His *gardener*? I don't know what part you've played in all this, or what you mean to that woman, but you standing here now tells me plenty. I always suspected you knew why that nasty, hateful woman left my brother and ruined our lives, and said nothing. I thank you for bringing the child. She's all I have left of Andrew."

"Can I say goodbye?"

"Wake her? Do you really think that's wise?"

Evie Lutyen shut the door and a passing air-raid warden told him to look lively there.

*Clematis occidentalis*

# 1947

On Thursdays, Rain caught the matinee at the Sphinx Theatre on Ventura. The young woman in the ticket booth always slipped him back a quarter. "Doesn't seem right charging you full price," she said once, "since you only come to see the newsreels, and why watch those? Nothing but bombed out cities and orphans. Enough to make you think the war was still on." She'd rather see that dreamy Tyrone Power any day.

Finding ticket stubs littered about Rain's kitchen, which was her office, Helen would coyly remind him how much she loved going to movies. Maybe they could do a matinee, but nothing like *Great Expectations*. Helen didn't like Dickens. His sentences had too many words and those happy endings got too nicely tied up. How about *The Harvey Girls*? If Helen had to come back in another life, she'd be Judy Garland—at least sing like her. Or maybe Gene Tierney.

But they never went. Helen wouldn't understand that it wasn't about seeing the movie. That he sat there looking desperately for a single face chanced upon in a newsreel crowd.

That Thursday afternoon, Rain drove his truck up the long drive to George Cukor's house high in the West Hollywood hills where below, Los Angeles rolled out like a quilt to the sea, passing

under the ancient eucalyptus as the heads of cream-coloured
sutera and morning glories nodded and fluttered in the garden
beyond. George adored the old grandeur of the towering eucalyptus, with its sweeping silvery-green crown, which meant he
had refused on several occasions to let Rain chop it down, even
if, as Rain argued, in dry spells, eucalyptus were famous for
dropping their heavy limbs without warning.

Helen was desperate to tag along on one of the Thursdays
when Rain touched up the Cukor garden. The director's glit-
tering parties had made centre spread in *Photoplay,* and Helen
was sure that if she could just get herself past the gate, she'd fill
plenty more pages in her autograph book. Too bad about what
happened to those Jews in Europe, she told Rain as she flipped
through the magazine, but the ones in Hollywood like George
sure weren't suffering.

Rain normally didn't see the director this early in the afternoon, so he was surprised to find him out back by the pool in a
short-sleeve shirt, the ice cubes in his glass fresh enough to clink.

"Just some folks over for lunch, nothing fancy," George said
by way of hello, "but you go on about your work. No one'll care
you're here."

The cars pulling alongside Cordell Drive began disgorging
thin legs and broad shoulders, faces desperately clinging to youth,
whether by makeup or the help of a surgeon. Rain envied their
head-tossing laughter and perfect white teeth, but their broad
smiles looked pasted on.

"Now hear me out," George said, trailing Rain around, "I
know you said you don't like doing movies, but I've got this
picture with Tracy and Hepburn you might be interested in."

Every week, the same plea. Some new picture with even
bigger stars. Rain was flattered of course, and he knew it was
crazy to think his gardens could last generations in a place like

Hollywood, but raking them over at the end of a film's shoot was too heartbreaking. Of course he didn't bother explaining that to George. "Thanks, Mr. Cukor, but I've got all the work I can handle right now."

Rain pulled a well-used handkerchief from his overall pocket and wiped his face. Thank God for that light breeze blowing as she walked down the curved stone ramp from the arbour. Big dark glasses framed her patrician face. She carried a drink in one hand. Her black hair was secured under a kerchief. She was not tall, and her generous curves were easily visible under her Capri pants and sleeveless blouse. At the bottom of the ramp, she kicked off her sandals, lit a cigarette, and eased onto a lounger. Then she removed her glasses and covered her eyes with the back of her arm.

"I watched you spend half an hour digging on your knees and talking magnolias with Vivien Leigh and you never broke a sweat," George said to Rain with a knowing chuckle. "Can it be that now you're star-struck?"

Certainly not, but she was Lena Lines, sitting right there. Like a real person. Breathing and everything. She'd just picked up her first Academy Award that spring for *Overruled by Heaven.* And, according to Hollywood, the world's most beautiful woman.

"See any of her films?"

Rain shook his head

"Dreadful. Of course, I didn't direct them," said George. "But to me, she'll always be Saint Bernadette. She was a teenager when she made that one, you know. Made her a star."

Lena removed her arm from over her eyes. "Georgie, you cocksucker, are you talking about me?"

The director managed the kind of smile Los Angeles was known for: the corners of the mouth went up, but the eyes didn't crease. "Just a word with the gardener."

"Is that the son-of-a-bitch who keeps this place for you? Come here. I'd get up, but I'm about to split my zipper."

The director practically had to pull Rain, all muddy denim and big loopy sweat stains under his arms, over to Lena.

The actress pushed herself off the lounger, downed the rest of her drink, and deposited the glass in George's hand. "We've got business, ya big ugly mutt," she said, taking hold of Rain's arm.

HELEN, TUCKED BEHIND HER DESK, surrounded by stacks of invoices and a potted mum needing water, hung up the phone.

"What's wrong?" asked Rain.

Her head shook, like someone else was moving it for her.

"Who was it?"

"Guy named Freddie," she said.

"Don't know him."

"Calling for Lena Lines."

*Oh.*

"You know her?"

"I'd rather know if the mail's here."

Helen rolled her eyes. It was always the mail with him. Lily, Lily, Lily. The least that woman could do was send a note, how hard could that be, well, if she wasn't dead, especially after Rain going all the way to France to help her out and having to come home through Spain and South America. South America! Didn't Rain know they had *cannibals*? Months of worrying over Rain getting shot at. Or eaten. Hardly a hair left on his head that wasn't grey, empty bottles on the table in the morning. How much sleep was he even getting? Then going back after the war! And just like Helen said he would, finding only rubble-filled lots and streets clogged with bricks, London a city of Displaced Persons that would take a decade to sort out. V for fucking Victory.

Gave himself a room in the hospital thank you very much and not one of his famous friends stopped by to see how his heart was doing. Well, thank God for Helen and her tea and toast and the bedside manner of a drill sergeant.

"Why didn't you say you knew her?" she asked.

"Who?"

"Lena Lines!"

"I don't, really. Met her at George Cukor's last Thursday."

"What's she like?"

"Nice." Foul-mouthed, too, but Rain didn't say.

Helen started getting up but the news was clearly too much for her and she slumped back into her chair. "No one tap dances quite like her, not even that Shirley Temple. Oh! Made we want to turn Catholic and be a nun when I saw *Saint Bernadette*. Did you see it?"

"The movie?"

"Her Academy Award."

"She doesn't carry it around with her. What did this Freddie want?"

"Oh, Lena wants to meet you. This afternoon. Lena Lines. You and her."


THE YOUNG MAN IN THE doorway had an impossibly tiny waist, very shiny hair, and clothes so tightly fitted that Rain wondered if he could sit down. The fellow couldn't have been more than nineteen or twenty, yet his cheeks and chin had a manly blue about them. You must be the gardener, was his greeting, sounding like he was rehearsing an exasperated Greta Garbo. "Miss Lines is out by the pool."

The muscles on the young man's face didn't move, except for a subtle flinch above the jaw. No one would ever mistake him for a labourer, like Rain, who should know better than to show up at her front door in rubber boots. There were service entrances for people like him. Rain felt he should apologize.

"Follow me."

From the interior of the house, Rain could see that Lena appreciated open spaces and lots of windows. Good to know if he was going to do her garden. Most of the furniture was low and square, easy and white. Painfully white. Did anyone ever sit on these sofas? No pets, naturally. The walls were covered in oversized, brilliantly colourful abstracts, a piercing black and white Ansel Adams portrait of Lena, and there were fresh cut flowers everywhere—bouquets of nodding peonies and hydrangea in pottery and crystal vases.

The patio doors opened onto a rectangular pool, watched over by towering Mediterranean cypress, where Lena was doing laps. On her head she wore a bathing cap covered in plastic daisies.

"Lovie, you're finally here."

Lena waved from mid-stroke then swam over to the side. She pulled herself out of the pool, naked, yanked off her bathing cap, and shook her shoulder-length black hair. "Hand me one, will you?"

Rain tried not to look as he pulled a thickly fleeced towel off the pile on the patio table.

She patted herself dry as the young man returned with a bottle of gin and an ice bucket.

"Cigarette?"

Rain shook his head.

Lena lit one for herself. Deep inhale. "Not scared off by a pair of tits, I hope."

The reappearance of the young man did not compel Lena to put on her robe.

"Freddie? Oh, he doesn't mind, do you lovie?"

The young man had only one facial expression.

"Freddie's the best houseboy I've ever had. Feast for the eyes, but a friend of Dorothy's."

Lena finally slipped on her robe. "Drink? You look like you could use one."

"It's early for me, Miss Lines."

"Don't you fucking *Miss Lines* me. It's Lena. Got it?"

Rain nodded as she handed him the gin-filled glass, no ice.

"Bottoms up, lovie, then you can drive me to the site."


LENA GOT INTO THE TRUCK wearing rubber boots, blue jeans and a yellow sweater, no more makeup that a hint of pink on her lips, and when she took off her sunglasses, she gave Rain those famously violet eyes that, according to Hollywood legend, had left both Gene Kelly and Kirk Douglas bedazzled. All together on the same night.

He pulled lunch wrappers and sketchpads off the passenger's seat of his truck. "You sure you want to drive over in this?"

"I grew up on a pig farm in Idaho with six brothers. We called this a Cadillac."

From her handbag, Lena pulled out a peanut butter and bacon sandwich, neatly wrapped in wax paper, and offered Rain half. What would Helen say about her idol when he told her?

"Like I was telling you, I don't want to live in a house that used to be someone else's. Real estate agents telling me this Spanish contemporary used to be James Cagney's pied-à-terre, or that Greek Revival was Bette Davis's love nest. As if I want to live in a house where that bitch got fucked. *Now, Voyageur* should have been mine, but—no, I want people to drive by my place and go, *oh, look, Lena Lines lived there.* You know, like they're at the Vatican."

Rain drove the truck past the Roman gates and up the drive bordered on one side by high walls resembling slices of wedding cake.

"And, lovie, you're just the man to help me do it."

To Rain, Lena's new eight-bedroom mansion was a jumbled mess of pitched-roof boxes, archways, and cloisters sheathed in stucco and capped with red tiles, all starkly perched on a hill overlooking Los Angeles.

"I've seen what you did for Georgie, so I know you can do what I want here."

He'd have his work cut out for him. Lena wanted large trees and mature vines over her terrace walls. "The house simply must look like it's been here for a couple of hundred years, you know, like those places in Venice." Two faux-rustic ponds on different levels were to drain into the swimming pool. The grounds would also have a tennis court, since Lena excelled at tennis and it kept her fit. She also wanted a series of outdoor rooms all connected with brick walks, so guests could take advantage of the views during parties. As for the type of plants, Rain could figure that out, after all he was getting paid to do something.

As they walked and Lena talked, Rain took notes and stopped here and there to make some hasty sketches. When was she going to mention her husband? Lena never talked about him. In Rain's experience wives called the shots to a point—then the husband reared his head, claimed he hadn't seen a single plan, and demanded major changes or Rain wasn't getting paid a cent.

"Does Mr. Mercy have any ideas I should know about?"

"Lovie, you do know how to ruin a gal's moment in the sun."

Rain knew nothing about the man other than what Helen had told him.

Imagine, Lena Lines and Randolph Mercy. Together. He put teenage girls into a swoon before the war, and when that style of crooning didn't sell records anymore, a minor role in a war film got him a nod from the Academy and a whole new career. Their wedding warranted a *LIFE* magazine special edition.

"That cheating bastard's doing a concert in New York and the only thing he's going to have to do with this place is pay for it."

LENA AND RAIN MET SOMETIMES for lunch, occasionally for dinner. Once they got photographed running to his truck and Lena joked that they'd be Walter Winchell's lead story: "Lena Lines's Secret Lover?" Rain didn't think so. Lena liked to surround herself with men the press wouldn't write about.

Helen remained desperate to know anything about her—what she wore, her perfume, how she talked.

"She's colourful," Rain said diplomatically.

His final plans for Lena's new house included trucking in eighty-two full-grown Italian cypresses and thirty-seven oaks. Vines woven with purple and white flowering clematis would thankfully conceal the wedding cake wall of the driveway terrace. Each of the elements painstakingly creating the lavish and casual retreat she wanted. The sweeping stone stairs from the back of the house would descend under a canopy of shade trees to the pool, where the back terrace and fountain would be left open, surrounded with trimmed boxwood to leave the city view unimpeded.

But Rain balked when Lena demanded a full-size showstopper like the one she adored at the Cukor house. "You know the Australians call that tree a widow-maker," he said. "Those eucalyptus can drop limbs in a drought, and it gets dry here in the summer. I'm not planting something that might come down through the roof."

Lena laughed like she did when she used to wrestle on the Idaho farm with her brothers. "Lovie, I had that name *long* before some dumb ol' tree in Australia." But she conceded, nonetheless.

Once he was finished with the rock-lined walks and hidden groves of unpredictably mismatched trees skirting the sunny views, her house would indeed look like it had been perched over the city long before movie folk had made California their home. It would be Rain's most expensive installation, and while Lena always waved off any talk of money, he wondered what she'd say when he handed her the bill.

THE DRIVEWAY TO LENA'S WELL-LIT Bel-Air place was full of cars when Rain arrived several days later with a sheaf of outstanding invoices for the garden over at her new house.

"Is this it? Is this where she lives?" asked Helen, straining to see through the truck's window.

The front door was open, light jazz was playing, glasses were tinkling in the early evening.

"I should have called first," said Rain, blocking in the Cadillac by the front door. "Let me see if I can find Freddie and leave the bills with him."

"Lovie!"

Lena saw his truck through the open door and hurried out, spilling whatever was in her glass. The event was pretty low-key judging from Lena's polka dot skirt and unbuttoned white blouse, which barely held everything back.

"Sorry, Lena. I was just driving my assistant home and thought I'd drop these off. Didn't mean to intrude."

"Wonderful, I'm sure. We can talk dollars later. Now get out of that truck and get in here, the both of you."

Helen, beaming, was already on the porch, quivering like she had to pee.

Lena took Rain's arm. "Look, lovie, Bill Remus brought over the rough cut of my new picture. Everyone in there is going to say they love it, but I know you'll tell me the truth." She leaned in closely. "I'm afraid it stinks."

Freddie, carrying a tray of drinks, stopped to give Helen the once over.

"We're not dressed for this." Rain usually waited outside clutching his straw hat when he came by.

"Lovie, nobody's here to see *you*. Speaking of which, you all right? Looking pale."

Rain had no time to reply. A woman wearing trousers with her hair in a brush cut and cowlick grabbed Lena's other arm and together they entered the screening room.

"She's got her own movie theatre," said Helen, every word coming out like a slow-melting caramel.

The woman clutching Lena's arm wasn't about to let go any time soon, but Lena glanced over her shoulder and motioned to them to sit behind her.

"Do you want something to drink?" Freddie looked as if there might be trouble if Rain said yes.

"Oh sure," said Helen. "I'll have a Singapore Sling. You do know how to make them, right?"

"You must be Helen," Freddie said. "Yes. We've spoken on the phone."

Oddly, they'd become the best of friends.

The windows of the outer wall were covered entirely with drapes that thankfully still allowed a cooling evening breeze, perfumed with citrus. Lena loved her lemons. Still, Rain took out a handkerchief and dabbed around his neck.

"Warm in here, huh?"

Helen didn't think so, but she was too excited to care.

The shorthaired woman tapped out a couple of cigarettes. Lena said she was trying to cut down, then said what the hell and took one.

"So out of the blue, Norman calls me."

"Blume?" asked Lena.

The friend nodded and snapped her fingers at Freddie, who was looking up Helen's drink in a book of cocktails, to bring them over something to use as an ashtray.

"Dee, I told you, never speak of that bastard again," said Lena.

"As your agent, it's my job to ignore you. He's over at Vox Pictures, you know."

"MGM gave him the boot? Good."

Even though the seats were wide and cushioned, Rain still felt confined. Maybe when the lights went down he and Helen could sneak out to his truck, although he doubted she'd go willingly. Lena would never notice. She was just being polite anyhow.

"You've got to let go of that *Wizard of Oz* thing, sweetie."

"That part was mine, Dee, and you know it."

"Lena, no one else in this town will tell you, but back then? You and your tits were too big to play a sixteen-year-old."

Lena took a deep drag on her cigarette. "You're my dearest friend, and a helluvan agent, but I hope your car slams into a lamppost on the way home tonight."

"No worries. I got your boy to make me up a room here, sweetie."

Lena's director, Bill Remus, the man looking very much like an accountant in his sweater vest and rimmed glasses, stood up before the front row. "We're ready, Lena."

She fluttered a few fingers back and Bill nodded to Freddie in the projection booth; he was doing double duty that evening.

"Norm wants you for a picture, Lena," Dee hissed over the noise.

"Did hell freeze over?"

"A big picture."

"Has your hearing been checked lately, Dee?"

The room went dark.

"It's rough, Lena," Bill yelled from the front row, "but you'll see, your best ever. Another Academy Award." In the light beaming from the projector, the director anticipated the victory with a raised glass.

A grainy black and white circle cut with an X flickered on the screen, then some upside down letters. Crackling came from the speakers around the room. Trumpets blared a march along with the title: *The New Official Films Present News Review of 1948.*

"Fuck, Bill, you know I hate the reels."

"Sorry, Lena. It's a mistake. I'll have a word with the editors."

On screen, two young women were being escorted across a schoolyard by a man who pointed out things like windows and doors and babies in drab mothers' arms. A throng of toothy, hungry-looking children waving British flags made out of paper cheered in the background.

*Two years after the war and England and Europe continue to rebuild. Today, the young Princess Elizabeth and Princess Margaret visit a newly rebuilt school, destroyed during the London Blitz.*

"Lena, I'm telling you this is a serious offer."

"And I'm telling you, I'll not work for that prick again."

"Look, Vox has been on the rails to B pictures since Jolson cried for his mammy. They want back on top. Norman's convinced the studio to gamble on one big blockbuster to turn things around."

"Go on, you're dying to tell me."

"They want to remake *Marie Antoinette.* Got Norma Shearer a nomination in '38."

"A period picture? Are you nuts, Dee? I don't do period. Me, strap these dogs into a corset for a month?"

"Hear me out. Period pictures are drawing crowds. People are tired from the war; they want to put all that foolishness behind them. Big, lavish, and Technicolor. Think about it. You. Tech-ni-color." Dee leaned close to Lena. "*Lenore* is your last contract picture. You're free to do this—at any price."

"But Normie Blume as producer?"

"Any price."

"Princess Margaret is so pretty," said Helen. "Much prettier than her sister, don't you think? Only the pretty ones should be queens."

On screen, the black and white images of happy workmen fitting pipes into high street shops turned over to the low smoky Parisian skyline dominated by the Eiffel Tower.

*In the birthplace of Robespierre, the Fourth Republic has taken over from the French postwar provisional government and tries to keep order where Nazi sympathizers on the run can still face the wrath of the people.*

A couple were being roughly handled on-screen by a crowd in a cobbled town square, the man beaten, bloody, the woman's dress torn and her long hair being roughly shorn. The man curled on the ground and looked to be pleading. The woman fought back hard, screaming, her arms pinned.

*A former Vichy government minister and his mistress on their way to Paris to face a trial for their role in mass deportations to Auschwitz are pulled by an angry mob from their car.*

"The bastard owes me a musical. If Norman wants me to do a picture with him, tell him it's got to be a musical."

Rain squirmed in that damned too-small seat, shut his eyes. But he could still see her. The woman, on her knees, clawing at the blades of those women cutting her, beating her, her hands shielding her bald and bloody shame. Air, he needed air. How can you not breathe in a room full of open windows?

Helen sat up, took his hand. "You okay?"

"All right, Lena. I'll see what Norm's got to say."

"Oh, and a million dollars."

"What?"

"A million. That's what I want to be in his movie."

"Lena, no actress ever got that much for one movie."

"If Vox wants me strapped into a corset for a month to save their Hymie asses, it's going to cost them. One million dollars."

On screen, ropes appeared from the crowd and were hastily tied around the man's neck. The woman's eyes rolled in terror, her open mouth screamed wordlessly under the narration. A searing, silent pain screamed inside Rain's chest—yet his eyes stayed fixed to the screen as the man was hoisted up, legs flailing, and hanged by his neck from the streetlamp in the square.

"Jesus," said Dee. "Can you believe the shit they put in these newsreels?"

RAIN OPENED HIS EYES TO two women looking down on him. Prim white hats perched on their heads like children's paper boats. Gardenias, roses, and gladiolus overflowed white wicker floor stands beyond.

"He doesn't look famous, but you know me, I don't get out to the movies as often as you."

"I've never seen him either, but he must be somebody. Maybe he's her director."

"Could be one of those stuntmen. That'll explain the face."

"No, I don't think so. They're quite fit."

"What's she like?"

"Nice as pie, like a regular person. And, oh my heavens, so beautiful—even though she had that scarf on, and those big sunglasses. Left the flowers. Must have cost a pretty penny. Gave me an autograph too."

"No!"

"I love her movies."

The two nurses looked back down at Rain.

"She was very concerned about him. Wanted to know what the doctor said and of course I had to say I couldn't tell her, but I did. Just that it was a heart attack and he should be all right, although it wouldn't hurt him to lose a few pounds. It was Lena Lines asking, for heaven's sake."

"Don't you worry, dear. I'd have done the same thing."


HELEN WAS FLIPPING THROUGH A magazine by Rain's hospital bed the next time he awoke. She nodded at the flowers at his bedside, fit for a Derby winner.

"Before you ask, I didn't get you those. Like Aunt Lucile says, no point in carrying coal to Newcastle. *She* sent them."

"Who?"

"Lena."

"You've changed your tune."

"Yes, she's clearly working you too hard."

Rain tried to sit up but realized he was hooked to more pieces of equipment than he could see.

"Don't blame Lena."

"No? All those hours you've been putting in on that new house of hers—"

"It's Lily. I saw her. On that newsreel."

The flipping magazine went silent.

"She's alive, Helen."

"Stop it. You've done everything you could to help her and almost killed yourself. Now look at you, right back here. If it *was* her—and it's probably just something you've made up in your head—I'm glad. Collaborating with Nazis? She got what she deserved."

"Lily wasn't smart enough for that, but Pierre was. If she's alive, maybe Nora is."

"You saw London. Miracle for anyone to survive. The girl probably didn't make it."

She was seventeen now. Maybe the doctor could give him something to dull the pain in his chest. A needle, morphine, right to his heart. "You can't talk to me like this."

Helen stood. "Somebody has to. If something happens to you, well, then I won't have a job."

After she was gone, Rain noticed the mug and plate of toasted bread on the side table and the small bouquet of carnations tossed in the wastebasket.

*Salix babylonica*

# 1951

Three horseback riders raced eternally in place across the desert. A young woman clung to the waist of the second, the bottom half of her face veiled, wistful eyes glancing back at a distant grove of palms. The detail on the stone relief panel was exquisite, and in pieces.

"Damn it," said Rain, tossing the crowbar to the floor.

Helen hurried over to the crate, glasses on her head, hands juggling invoices. "I did tell you not to order from that company. No way that's going back together. Those English're selling off anything not nailed to the floor to make ends meet. Look what it gets you."

Broken marble on a bed of straw. The panel had been meant to be fitted with a spigot, and turned into a wall fountain.

"It'll be weeks, *months*, before I can find a replacement," Rain said, frustrated. "Then who knows how long on a ship." *Time. Time. Time.*

"You're the one who's always saying a garden can't be rushed." Helen went back to the paperwork. "And no one'll be the wiser if you get one slapped together down in Mexico. By the way, that Winston woman called again this morning."

"Who?"

"Marjorie Winston. Very insistent. Says you two go way back. Seems to think you're the only gardener in town. I told her you're too busy, which is true if you want to know what I think—"

"Which I don't."

"You should be taking it easy."

"I'm fine," he said.

"Your heart and the doctors have a different opinion." Helen pushed her hair back, determined to make sense of why she was being charged so much. "She was married to that congressman."

"Who?"

"Marjorie Winston! Had something to do with the State Department, or Immigration, getting refugees over here after the war. Remember? He was killed in that plane crash a few years ago. Spain I think."

"How do you know these things?"

She slapped her thigh. "I'm not just a nice set of gams. I do read the newspapers now and then. She'll want her garden done in time for her fundraiser. She's a big Democrat."

Rain continued to stare at the broken marble. "Did you say her husband was a congressman?"

"Huh?"

"Give me her address. I'll drive over and see what she wants."

"Now?"

MARJORIE WINSTON STOOD ON HER head by the pool of her Long Beach home.

"You ought to give it a try. A wonder for wrinkles." She slapped her chin with the back of her hands. "No reason why even you can't look your best."

She did have a remarkably unlined face, which Rain suspected was more a testament to her surgeon's skill than to headstands.

Still, considering the closely guarded secret of her age, it was no small feat. She kept herself trim and wore a two-piece bathing suit. Her white hair had a blue tinge and a conspicuous strand of pearls kept her neck taught.

Marjorie pulled a thin cotton shift about her shoulders, gestured to a seat under a shading acacia as Rain looked over the adobe hodgepodge of arches and iron balconies enclosing the pool. Otherwise the garden was quaintly classic with its trimmed borders and gold and copper marigolds.

A young, well-muscled man in bathing trunks bounced from the house with a tray of drinks. He plunked the tray down, then hopped into the seat beside Marjorie as if it were a hurdle. She in turn rubbed the back of his hand.

"Thanks, pet." She turned her attention back to Rain. "Been a long time."

A lot of miles since Paris, but Marjorie wasn't one to look back.

"I adored what you did with my dear friend George's place in West Hollywood. Loved that house. That garden of yours was magnificent. You've done all right for yourself." She offered him a glass short on ice and long on bourbon. "Heard George sold that place to Milton Berle. Dreadful man. Dresses up in women's clothing. On television. They say he's going to tear it down and built apartments. Do hope he leaves that exquisite eucalyptus."

In the minutes before she had to dash after her nearly naked pool boy and dress for a dinner party, Rain had sketched out, for her approval, a sandstone walk flanking a canal with modish water jets. On one side, olive trees planted in sunken parterres to be surrounded by rotating annuals, the heads of which would be at the same level as the walk. On the other side, hydrangea trees against a wall of yews would provide a canopy for beds of yellow and red sedum. A giant palm, set slightly off-angle against the corner cloisters, would anchor the garden, and Rain knew just where to find it. A woman in the valley owned acres of mature trees he'd been purchasing over the years. In he'd come with a cheque, and out he'd go soon after with a nice specimen on the back of his flatbed.

"I hate to talk money, it's so vulgar. Why don't you write down on that paper of yours how much all this is going to cost. If I don't have a coronary, we'll have a deal."

"Maybe it doesn't have to cost you anything."

Marjorie looked at him blankly, then laughed. "Oh, honey, I'm flattered, really I am. But you saw Marco—"

"No, no! Not that. I wanted to ask about your late husband."

"Stanford?"

"Is it true he worked for the government?"

"Ah, yes, yes he did."

"You still have connections?"

"I hadn't taken you for the political sort."

"Do you?"

"High hopes for Congressman Kennedy. So I want this garden ready for a party I'm hosting—"

"I need help finding someone. Overseas. I've tried everything I know, officially, for the last few years with no luck. Everyone thinks I'm crazy."

"Are you?"

"I know she's alive." *Both of them.*

Marjorie fingered her pearls absent-mindedly. "And you think I can help?"

"I'm desperate."

A top up of the bourbon, and a think, was necessary.

"You know, my husband was many things being a politician, not many of them virtuous, but one thing he *was* good at, was knowing it's best to leave a party or political office before it's over.

*Marj*, he'd say to me, *there's power in goodbye*. Of course, he also meant our marriage. But if you've already tried everything, maybe who you're looking for shouldn't be found."

Rain drained the last of his bourbon, stared at the almost melted ice swirling around the bottom and held his breath. "Please."

Marjorie gazed out over the pool. "It won't be cheap."

"I'll do the garden. No charge."

"That's a given, dear."

"Mooning after that Lily put you in the hospital for weeks," Helen said, so angry Rain thought she might cry in front of him, for the first time ever. "And where was she? By your bedside making sure you didn't die? No! That was me. I thought she was out of your system. Now here you are, taking on even more work—for free! You'll be right back in the hospital, but I tell you this, don't expect me to be there. Or help you. You want to work for nothing, that's your business, but I don't."

Rain knew she would.

The gate to his backyard slammed after Helen, leaving him alone with a beer and a cigarette by the empty pool.

*Damn it.*

The ringing phone inside was not going to stop. Rain groaned as he stood, his lower back unhappy at the exertion. He hated getting old. His body felt like it was rebelling, joint by joint, aching where it never used to. Places that Doctor Elliot had stitched up years ago that had barely bothered him were acting up too.

It was Lena.

"Is that you, lovie? Good. You're home. I'll be 'round in half an hour. We're going for a drive."

LENA ARRIVED WRAPPED in a scarf and oversized glasses two hours later. Her Buick convertible was obvious and shiny.

"Vulgar, I know, but that's why I love it. Don't stand there gawking. Hop in."

When Rain did, Lena removed her glasses.

"Let me look at you, you big ugly mutt."

She kissed him on the cheek, then pulled away from the curb with a roar.

"Jesus, lovie, you can't even see your place from the street. Don't you own pruning shears or something? Not what I expected from the man who found me my Monterey pines."

Yes, only six weeks after his heart attack, Helen fussing, he'd overseen the installation of those trees, a hundred years old if a day, a thousand bucks a piece. Reminded him of those oak saplings back in France, at Bon Sauveur. How big would they be now?

"Where are we going?"

"Just sit back and let me thank you for what you did at my house. Being home these last few weeks, I've enjoyed that glorious garden of yours for the first time. Everyone loves it, but that doesn't mean I'm not angry with you. Why haven't you called?"

"I finished the job."

"But I thought we were friends, lovie? Christ knows I've got few of those here and none like you. Never thought I could just be *friends* with a man, you know, without the screwing and all, but it's not like you'd ever think about that." She patted his thigh. "We clear?"

Rain nodded, feeling scolded.

"Good. Now, how's that heart of yours doin'?"

"Helen keeps an eye on me."

"That girl still with you, huh?"

"She's good at what she does."

"You're loyal, I'll give you that. Me? I'd have ditched the sour-faced cow a long time ago. A face like hers could turn a bowl of cream to curds. She's in love with you, you know that, right?"

*Helen? No.* Helen would want a man who.... Actually, he had no idea what Helen wanted.

But Lena wanted to talk about Lena. "I suppose you've heard."

"Only what's been in the papers. Helen keeps me informed." *Daily.*

Lena veered without looking onto the freeway. "Oh, lovie, they've only got it half right."

"Read about you being sick."

Rain had seen the photo of Lena carried off the plane in a wheelchair.

"You mean this?" She pulled her scarf down and felt the base of her throat. "Should have known a simple thing like a cold would turn into pneumonia in that God-forsaken country. The British do not understand the concept of central heating, but yes, I suppose if you need a tracheotomy, best get sick at a hotel full of drunk medical students."

Lena laughed like a man, deep and rough.

"When do you go back to London?"

"Not going back. It'll be in *Variety* tomorrow. Vox is moving the picture here. Finally took that idiot producer off the project, too. It was Blume's idea to film in London in the first place. Spends half a million dollars to build Paris on twenty acres in a country that's soaking wet. You have no idea how many days shooting we wasted waiting for the sun."

A milk truck honked as it roared past. Lena waved. She wasn't the best at staying in a lane. They flew past a rusting neon sign in the shape of a curvaceous waitress holding up a tray of burgers.

"The thing is, I'm the star. If *Marie!* goes down the crapper, it'll be me everyone blames. So I called up the head of Vox and told him, I want a new script, new songs, and Sam Boullian out of retirement to direct."

"And they agreed?"

"I'm Lena Lines, lovie."

Just past Chatsworth, Lena turned the car off the pavement and onto a dirt road leading into scrubby dry hills, oblivious to the stones pinging off her shiny new convertible. Wherever they were, there wasn't much to see, though it did look vaguely familiar. Rain had been here before. Years ago now, with Florence Yoch when she was finishing that picture set in China. This was MGM country.

"Not much farther," Lena said.

She stuck one hand out of the window and let her fingers catch the wind. Considering the condition of the road, Rain wished she'd keep both hands on the wheel.

A few miles up, Lena waved to the parked car ahead, where three men were looking over unrolled diagrams covering the hood, their edges held down with stones. The oldest fellow, in his sixties, balding, portly in a grandfatherly sort of way, who made a uniform of Hawaiian print shirts open down to his belly, was carving an apple with a penknife, then popping the pieces into his mouth. The two younger men occasionally glanced cautiously at the rolling hills behind them.

"Lena, my dear." The man in the Hawaiian shirt, Sam Boullian, wrapped her in a bear hug. The two other men he introduced as the new art director and production designer for *Marie!*

"Is this your guy?"

Lena tucked her arm through Rain's. "Sammy, don't judge the book by the cover."

Another piece of apple went into the director's mouth. "All right, what do you think?"

Rain didn't know what he was supposed to think.

"Sure, today dusty hills and coyotes in the San Fernando Valley, but tomorrow, the place'll be crawling with heavy equipment."

Sam grandly gestured to the future site of eighteenth-century Versailles. The plans on the hood of the car also called for the Orangery with the staircase of One Hundred Steps, the Queen's Grove, the Menagerie, Grand Trianon, and the Fountain of Neptune. "And here." Sam tapped the blueprint. "A grand view down the Royal Avenue to the Fountain of Apollo. How big?"

"A hundred and seventy acres," said the production designer.

"That's right. Bigger than the real thing, my man. Nothing's too grand for our Lena."

"The gardens of Versailles in the eighteenth century were a hundred times larger."

"What? You don't say?"

Lena laughed. "Told you I was right about him."

Rain bent low and looked at the drawings, "What does this have to do with me?"

"When people come to see this movie, I want them to be ooh-ing and ah-ing. Jesus-fucking-Christ, everyone knows about Versailles. My garden has to be better than the real thing. Second billing to our star here." Boullian nodded towards Lena. "I hear you're the man for the job."

Rain felt Lena's breasts against his arm as she looked over the plans too.

The art director and production designer weren't so transfixed. Rain guessed what they were thinking.

"One and a half million budget for the set," Boullian added.

"Finding the plants that were used, recreating—"

"Screw that. All the camera needs is trees and fountains. Make it look sensational. Can you do it?" The last piece of apple went into Sam's mouth.

"Of course he'll do it, won't you, lovie?"

"You're in a good mood," Helen said, looking out the window as Rain drove the truck up the steeply rising, slightly curving lane and came to a stop. Boxwood lined the driveway and mature sycamores screened the neighbouring North Pasadena properties. "Hey. I thought you said lunch."

"We will."

"Place looks familiar," she said. "We do something here?"

"Yup. A few years ago."

The green canopy parted at the top of the driveway where the red house with its white-painted brick chimney appeared to float in borders of rose and seafoam *crème de la crème* phlox.

"Yeah. I remember now. Never did like this place."

Rain stepped out of the truck and tried not to smile.

"Who has a pathway that doesn't go to the front door? You're supposed to park by the front door and walk into a house, not detour by the pool. And who in their right mind would build on the side of a hill?"

But Rain preferred to enter the property from the curved lot in front of the garage, with its office over the top, then walk through the grove of crabapples, past a guava and a Japanese maple planted to look like it had broken through the foundation, to the delightful house with its cheery windows and varying rooflines that blended naturally with the well-treed lot. Stone walks surrounded the house and led to paths and wooden benches overlooking the mountain views, and down to the formal pool shaded by magnolias, cypress, and cycads.

Here and there, large, unmatched clay pots overflowing with hosta, the broken remains of a brick wall, and an ivy-covered Greek god that should have looked ridiculously out of place, but didn't.

"C'mon," he said, walking up to the house. "No one's home."

"Why are we here?"

"I always loved this place. Peaceful and simple. Perfect place to raise a family. Maybe even a puppy."

"Okay...owners want you to come back and do something?"

"No. Just wanted to see how our garden held up."

At the large latticed window, Rain peered into the living room.

"Hey, you sure nobody's home?"

Helen glanced around but Rain's landscaping ensured privacy from the nearby houses. "Hope there's no guard dog." She studied Rain suspiciously. He seemed happier than she'd seen him...well, ever.

"I have a confession to make," Rain said, leading Helen down the steps to the pool. "I've made on offer."

"On what?"

"This house."

"To buy this *house*?"

"Yes!"

"Are you...how—why?"

"Like I told you, of all the places I've done, this is the one... that felt like home. *My* home. It's me, Helen. But it's still a lot of house for one person."

"Oh, I see."

"There's something else I need to tell you."

Helen's faced reddened around a grin. She appeared flustered, as if the warm afternoon was making it hard for her breathe.

"I'm not sure how to tell you this."

"Spit it out, I always say."

"I found Lily and my—her Nora."

"What?"

"Actually, Marjorie Winston found them, through her husband's contacts at the State Department."

Helen's arms dropped to her side. Her sweater looked too big. The hard, feather-like leaves of the cycads nodded and rustled in the breeze from the San Rafael Hills.

"Helen, are you angry?"

"Of course not. Just didn't think it would happen...so soon. You want this woman and her daughter to live here? With you?"

"Yes, of course. At least—"

"What?"

"Until we...until they get settled. Figure out what to do next."

"How long will that be?"

"I don't know. Life hasn't been easy for them."

"Looks like they're about to land on their feet."

"Helen—"

She nodded at the house. "As the person who does your accounts, I can tell you, you can't afford it."

"I'll sell my place in San Gabriel."

"That dump? Won't even pay the taxes here."

Rain unwrapped the shabby blue and green scarf from his neck.

"Oh Jesus. I know that look. What else haven't you told me?"

"Lena asked me to do her movie."

"Are you crazy? You hate doing movies, and that one's going to be the biggest turkey this town's ever filmed. A musical about Marie Antoinette is the worst idea any producer's ever had. For Christ's sake, she gets her head chopped off at the end!"

"One movie, that's all. Like you said, I can't afford this house. I need to."

"By selling your soul to the devil." She turned and marched back towards the truck.

"Helen? Wait, where are you going?"

"Back to work. Can't waste all day out here. Specially now."

"What about lunch?"

"Save your money. You'll need it."

IN THE MORNINGS, Helen used to come round to Rain's bunga-low. She'd let herself in, turn on the radio, make coffee, fry up some eggs, and sort the day's business in the back room that looked out onto the empty pool. Then he signed onto *Marie!*, and moved into the new house, and now Helen waited for him by the studio gate, with coffee in paper cups. They had an office around the corner from the sound lots and the com-missary. Beside her desk were a few chairs for the production staff. Rain's room, at the top of the narrow stairs out back, was fitted with a levered drafting table and shelves for reference books. The walls steadily disappeared under Rain's photographs, sketches, prints, maps, lists of nurseries, and the ever-evolving production schedule.

His phone rang.

"Someone to see you."

Helen had taken some convincing to accept the job, and more to accept that she didn't have to come up the stairs every time she wanted to talk to him. *Use the phone*, he had said. When she did her tone was such that Rain wished he hadn't.

Rain saw two pairs of legs, from the knees down, as he descended the stairs. Then before him were two women: the older holding a suitcase and looking exhausted, the younger wearing a careless, angry beauty. Lily. Maybe thicker around the waist and very grey, but still her. And Nora, a young woman now, with very red lips. Nothing about the girl was familiar to Rain, not her face, not the colour of her hair, or the way she sat clutching her knapsack looking up at him, and yet—still he'd know her anywhere.

"What's wrong?" asked Helen from behind her desk.

Rain's hand absent-mindedly went to his chest, but not for the reason that had Helen dialling the studio infirmary.

"Put down the phone," he said.

"Been a long time," said Lily nervously, getting up.

*My darling thing.*

Rain thought he heard himself say, yes. A long time.

She moved towards him, as if she wanted to embrace, but something stopped her and she bit her bottom lip. Lily coughed then.

Her daughter handed her a handkerchief.

"No, I'm fine."

Helen offered to bring coffee, or juice, anything—maybe she just wanted to get away. "Might have told me they were coming today," she said on her way out.

"Look at you, all famous. I was telling Nora when we saw that picture in the magazine, you and that movie star, why he must be doing well."

The young woman dropped her knapsack on the ground and stood up, but remained apart. "I wasn't sure you'd remember me, Uncle."

He wanted to say that not a day went by when he didn't wonder if she'd been blown to bits, buried under rubble, or was alive somewhere, forgetting all about him. Now she stood right there, and that short space between them felt like the farthest apart they'd ever been.

Lily, looking small and neglected, clutched her handbag tightly.

"Now, see, I can tell us being here comes as a surprise."

"No, no. I didn't know you'd be here today, that's all. How long have you been in town?"

"Just got off the bus. Had to take a sponge bath in the lavatory." She laughed, short and quick, without looking at him. "Spent a fortune on taxis to get here, I can tell you that. But don't you worry. That nice government man who brought us took care of it."

Helen returned with refreshments to see them retreating across the parking lot towards Rain's truck.

"You've a meeting with the production designer," she called after him. "The Trianon set. Remember?"


RAIN LAY BY THE POOL and wriggled his bare feet, the lights of Pasadena brightening in the twilight. Faint music came from the house. He'd never really got the concept of lounging, which seemed to be a very California idea, but at least in this house he'd filled the pool. Filled the rooms with those he loved. Made them safe. *If I die right now, right this very moment, at least I've known happiness once in my life.* Perfectly content. Sin to want more. Afraid that even breathing would dispel such bliss.

Nora, his Nora, came down to the pool carrying two bottles of beer. It took some getting used to, seeing this young woman and not the child he had held in his heart all these years. Her hair was wet from her long bath and she'd changed into loose fitting trousers and a sweater.

"Nice view from up here. I take it from the boxes you've not been in long."

"I wanted you both to be comfortable."

"How thoughtful, Uncle."

"Your mother?"

"Sleeping. Found these in your refrigerator. Mind?"

"Guess I still think of you as a little girl." He took the offered beer and gestured to the empty lounge chair beside him.

"That's okay, pops." Nora drank from her bottle. "Do Americans really call their fathers that? Or would you prefer dad? How about poppa?"

"She told you."

"Not so much. Figured most of it out. Even the dearest uncle in the world wouldn't do what you did for me."

"I wanted you, but your aunt—"

"But she wasn't that, was she?"

"I went back for you as soon as I could."

She reached over and helped herself to one of Rain's cigarettes. "Relax. I stopped hating you a long time ago."

"The house was gone and no one knew where you were."

"Up north. Evie died in the Blitz."

"I'm sorry."

"I'm not. Spiteful, stubborn woman. Stayed on the street until we were the last house standing. Wouldn't go near the shelters and because the man I thought was my father never made it back from France, they shipped me and the other orphans to Scotland. Luckily, I got a family that never let me forget how grateful I should be for their charity." She chuckled, a bit ironically. "After the war I made my way back to London, got my name on the displaced persons list. That's how someone from your embassy finally found us, though getting Mama out of that French prison took some convincing."

Rain wiped his cheek as he watched Nora blow a long cloud of anger towards the sky.

"Jesus. You still love her, don't you? Don't say, it doesn't matter. Look, I don't know what you expect, bringing her here, but you should know, she's not well. What they did to her in France...even she won't talk about it. She acts all right most of the time, until she doesn't. Won't see a doctor either."

Didn't matter. Alcohol on an empty stomach making him lightheaded, the euphoric numbing shock. Joy in measures almost too painful to savour. Lily and Nora, his Lily, his Nora, safe. Everything he'd ever come to want. Here! With him. Home. He just wanted to hold her and feel that she was real.

"It must have been hard for her, and for you."

"For Christ's sake," Nora said, drawing heavily on her cigarette and tossing back the last of her beer.

FOR THOSE FIRST FEW DAYS Lily slept. When she did appear, Rain thought her confused, as if she were only pretending to understand what was being explained to her. She wore a kerchief over her head, but Rain could see the handfuls of hair falling out. She balked at any suggestion that she should see a doctor, and was easy to anger. And no, she shot back with a wave of her hand, she damn well *didn't* want to talk about Paris, or Walling, or fucking anything else. She was in America now. What did she care about the past? Why remember? What good had any of it done her?

Maybe sitting around wasn't such a good idea. Rain thought Nora and her mother might want to unpack the moving boxes that were scattered about the house, make the place feel more like a home. They remained untouched. The man from the liquor store called and said the two women at that address had run out Rain's account. Nora turned her nose up at going back to school, the idea of college. She had all the education she needed, thanks pops.

"I just have to be patient. They need more time to settle in," Rain told Helen as if trying to convince himself.

More of *his* time, Helen corrected, but as she reminded Rain, he'd made that deal with the devil.

And though it pained him to admit it, she was right. The production of *Marie!* was demanding more and more of each day.

"*Assistant?*"

"It's a wonderful opportunity, Lily. Lena's a great actress and my friend." Privately, Rain suspected that Lena never did a kindness without a motive, but that was beside the point. "Nora will learn a lot."

"How to fetch coffee and God knows what else. Look at your daughter. She's beautiful enough be a movie star. I can't believe you're making her an errand boy."

Lena had no reputation for benevolence, especially toward younger, prettier women. But in a town where an actress's currency equated to how willingly she'd spread her legs, Rain was thankful for Lena's offer.

"Everyone has to start somewhere, and Nora gets to work on the biggest picture in Hollywood right now. Anyone would think this is a wonderful opportunity."

Nora sat on a stool at the counter in Rain's kitchen, angrily leafing through one of Helen's issues of *Photoplay*. "Leave it, Mother. He's right," She glared at Rain. "Can't sit around here forever."

"Eight months today we've been working on this all-singing all-dancing turkey," said Helen with her gravelly smoker's voice, looking at the wall calendar covered with Xs.

She wore a scarf wrapped around her head under her wide-brimmed straw hat. Bathing her face in lemon juice to lighten the freckles wasn't working.

She handed Rain a Thermos of water.

He spit the grit from his mouth and blinked against the dry wind. "Let's get the trucks up here to wet things down before they shoot."

He turned at the sight of the dust cloud in the distance,

billowing in the wake of a convoy. "What's coming today?"

Helen consulted the clipboard. "Hyacinth, oculus-christi, violet juliennes, anemones, irises, crown imperials, sweet rockets, and ranunculi."

"We'll be lucky if half are alive by noon tomorrow."

"It's getting worse," she replied. "We've emptied nurseries for miles. Tried just over the border in Mexico. No luck."

"Costa Rica?"

"It'll be expensive. Have to ship them in. I mean, by boat."

"You heard Boullian," said Rain.

"But the budget?"

"Christ almighty. He doesn't care, why should we?"

They ate a hasty lunch as they redrew the plans for wooded groves filled with hissing waterworks, lulled by the Mexican migrant workers singing as they filled in the parterres around the chateau set with veronicas, pasque flowers, feverfews, tuberoses, white lilies, valerians, and jasmines. Then squeaking cranes lifted full-grown sycamores, sweet chestnuts, oaks, cypress, silver fir, lindens and larches, maples and hollies and white poplars, and those weeping willows by the ponds of Marie Antoinette's playground, Petit Trianon, into pre-dug holes.

"Reminds me, we're running out of water," Helen said.

"I know, I know."

"You working late tonight?"

Rain glanced at his watch. *Damn it.* He wanted to be home early. Lena kept Nora occupied, but Lily, bored and idle now for months, was drinking heavily and alone. With each outburst he cleaned up after, he loved her less and nursed her more.

"I still haven't got that view right," he said to Helen. "Those packages from France arrive?"

Helen spread out the etchings and old maps that would help them recreate the view from the Fountain of Neptune to the

Swiss Lake: the shot Sam Boullian needed to heighten his most important scene, the coronation.

Rain pondered the view. Nothing seemed to come easily these days. *The scale, how do I create the scale?* Helen's gaze was piercing. "But you go home," he said.

"Then here." She slammed a rifle across the tiny table in his trailer. "And before you get all high and mighty on me, the foreman says bobcats are coming down the hills after those rabbits out there eating everything you haven't covered in chicken wire. Don't leave here without it."

That night, as he fell asleep over the wheel, Rain's truck drifted off the deserted highway and slammed to a halt on the shoulder, sending leaves of crumpled paper out the windows, covered with furious notes about converging lines and narrowing the lake, all to create the illusion of distance.

DOZENS OF CREW, CAMERA OPERATORS, and costumed extras waited for the pennant to wave. When it did, jets hissed into the hot air, the mist softening the view: the boxwood curlicues clipped around the Three Fountains on the right, the mysterious grove shading the Arc de Triomphe on the left, and the Allée d'Eau all the way to the distant blue Swiss Lake.

Sam Boullian clapped. Everyone clapped. "Bravo! Bravo! Why, it looks like it goes on for miles. How did you do it?"

Before Rain could answer, a fast-moving truck roared onto the set in a spray of sand and gravel. The man from the nearby town, jumping out angrily, waved his arms at the spritzing fountains.

"Local mayor," Helen said, taking off her sunglasses as the man approached and wiping off the dust. "You should know, he's a bit of a hothead."

"You people! First you raid our orchards and vineyards for our workers. Now you take our water. Every time you turn on your goddamned fountains, our toilets don't flush!"


NONE OF THE STUDIO TRAILERS were air-conditioned so Rain started making excuses to stop by the onsite bungalow built for Lena, which included a full kitchen with cook and cathedral ceilings. On hot days like this it was the perfect place for her to shelter during her costume fittings. Lena stood, in a black brassiere and panties, cigarette in hand, as three women circled her with pins and tape measures and fitted what looked like an upside-down cane basket to her waist.

"Don't be ridiculous, lovie, of course come in. Have a drink."

Rain sat awkwardly on the large L-shaped sofa in front of her.

Lena wriggled her bottom and the basket shook. "It's a bloody wonder these people didn't have to turn sideways to enter a room."

Rain said the doors at Versailles, the real Versailles, were wide to accommodate the fashion.

"Aren't you just a walking encyclopedia of I-don't-give-a-fuck."

The women pinning stood back, shaking their heads unhappily.

"Help yourself," Lena said, from the pitcher of lemonade reeking of vodka on the coffee table. "I know you don't drop by to see me, but Nora's not here. So tell me, how'd it go by the lake?"

"Sam was happy. Ecstatic, actually."

"On the Paris set?"

"The extras play cards and grumble about the studio making them share paper cups to save money."

"They're getting paid, aren't they?"

"That's just it. Do you know how much I've spent on the gardens already? Does the studio know?"

"Don't worry," Lena said.

"Isn't Sam concerned about someone seeing the books?"

Lena brushed away her fussing handmaidens and flounced off the dais. She butted out her cigarette and poured herself a tall glass of lemonade.

"Look, lovie, I get that you're frustrated, I am too. But Sam's a fucking perfectionist and he's pulling this script out of the john. So he's rewriting it at night and shooting by day. Popping bennies by the handful. He's going to kill himself, but hopefully not before we're done. Not the best way to film, I agree, but those extras sitting around are getting paid to play poker. Between you and me, don't expect things to get better."

"How much longer?" Rain's garden wasn't made to last. "Can't keep up that water truce with the town forever."

"You can't walk out on me now, lovie."

But he worried. He wasn't getting to spend any time with Lily. Maybe it wasn't quite the happy family he'd hoped for, but if he could just get to the end of this production, whenever that would be, Rain felt sure he could make things right. For now, all he could do was justify the long days for the sake of Lily and his daughter.

"About her. I agreed to give the kid a job as a favour to you, but I'm telling you, that's one ungrateful little bitch. She's got a face as long as pulled taffy when she's here, and you see how busy I am. I can't be running around making sure she's got Sam's new script pages every morning."

Lena tossed back the rest of her lemonade and refilled the glass. "You know she's taken up with a gaffer. Nasty piece of rough I hear."

He didn't know. "She's a child."

"Lovie, that girl is no child."

THE SUNDAY SCHOOL NUNS of Rain's youth had got death all wrong. A man could die a thousand deaths and still be standing, still be breathing. No bright lights and Jesus holding a dove and peace and love and all that shit. Death can be pulling up into your driveway in the middle of the night to find the lights spilling out every window of your house, Dean Martin on full blast on the hi-fi. Inside: Lily, limp, barely standing, in the arms of a middle-aged Italian American in a dirty T-shirt, frothy chest hair peeking out from the neck, and an exceedingly black toupée. Rain a ridiculous empty sack of nothing-to-her standing stupid-faced in the doorway.

Lily laughed, then coughed enough for the pot-bellied man to go *whoa there, little lady,* and save her plunging to the floor, propping her back up in a chair.

"Meet Jay," said Lily. She stunk of whatever cheap liquor the two of them were drinking. "Fixes cars. Got himself a real job."

"It's late, Lily, and I have to get up early in the morning." *I'm doing this for you.*

See?" said Lily. "No fun, like I told you. Do *this* Lily, do *that* Lily, just be happy bored and boarded up with me, Lily. Like a sad old bull, mooning after me with those eyes, always telling me what to do. Look at him, like bloody Frankenstein. Jay, honey, you know someplace we can go, just the two of us?"

The mechanic laughed, patted Rain on the back. "Just adore your little lady's accent. All posh-like."

"Lily, it's time for your friend to go. You've had enough."

She dragged a half-empty bottle across the counter towards her, then pulled herself off the chair. Rain hardly recognized her.

"Don't tell me what to do. Y'always telling me what to do. But he can't do anything himself. Not like you, Jay. I ask for one thing, just *one thing*, get my poor sweet Nora into the movies. Make her a star. She's beautiful enough to be in the movies! Make lots of money so we can get out of this dump." She pounded Rain's chest weakly with the bottom of the bottle. "Jay can do it. He knows a studio in North Hollywood, makes art films. S'gonna make Nora a star."

Rain grabbed Lily's arm. "Art films? I know all about those North Hollywood studios. Pornography, Lily. You want your daughter taking off her clothes for the camera?" He reached for the telephone.

"Hey, what are you doing?" she asked with a hacking laugh.

"Calling the police. Bet they'd like to know what Jay here is up to."

Turns out Jay wasn't so very drunk. His big, meaty hand ripped the phone easily from Rain, dragged him with some difficulty through the hall to the back door, and threw him down steps to the lower lawn. Lily crying, screaming, tossing bottles, neighbours' lights flicking on. Rain went easily into the pool. The splash was big. He hadn't swum since that night in the river. *Since Euan.* Coughing, sputtering, drowning. And for what? Nothing had changed.

"Oh, my dear thing," sobbed Lily, on her knees by the edge. "Now look at you. This isn't my fault. None of this is my fault. You want too much. You always wanted, too much."

At least she stayed around long enough to make sure he could float.

WHEN HELEN ARRIVED at the hilltop house she had never cared for, and probably cared for even less now what with Lily and Nora being around, she found Rain sitting in his kitchen, his wet clothes dripping on the floor. Empty bottles covered the counter, a chair lay sideways, the windows needed opening to air out the stench of stale tobacco. Broken glass crunched under her feet. But with the look on his face, there was no way she was going to ask what had happened.

"Early for you to be in the pool," she said, trying to find someplace to put down the bag of breakfast. "No bathing suit?"

Without looking at her, he managed, "She's gone."

*For good,* he figured.

He'd finally got the message. What a stupid, stupid fool he'd been. He had hoped for so long that his love could be enough for them both, that one day she'd say she loved him back and that he'd come to believe it. That she would truly be his Lily. But all he'd done, all these years, was force her into a debt she had no ability to repay, with no way to say *I can't love you.* If only she'd put him out of his misery years ago. If only he had read the signs. Well, she had finally done it, with Jay and his toupée and his chest hair and faded charm and greasy nails, and a remorseless peel of laughter that pierced his bleeding heart.

Helen picked up the chair, started sweeping the broken glass. Thankfully she refrained from giving her two cents over something even a jackass could have seen coming. Early sun pushed through the kitchen window. Another hot day ahead.

"Get some dry clothes," she said. "I'll make coffee."

The casualties at Versailles would be mounting.

RAIN BEGAN HIS DAYS WALKING the movie set avenues making sure they were free of kingsnakes and coachwhips. Snakes loved the heat. Lena did not like snakes. The ponds were greening over with algae and had to be drained and scrubbed. By now his crew was replacing wilting trees and replanting flowers daily in case the cameras rolled. The set needed its own plant nursery.

A truck was kept on site, expensively fitted with a giant spade to scoop out dead trees and drop in new ones. Flowers were kept in hundreds of clay pots so they could be more easily replanted. Even so, there was trouble finding suitable replacements. Without telling Boullian, Rain had the Property Department painstakingly wrap thousands of handmade silk blossoms and artificial fruit to tree limbs. They looked so lifelike that Rain had once watched a starling in a frantic tug-of-war with a rubber grape.

The most complicated and lengthy scene to film was the coronation sequence. It took Boullian five days to shoot, during which time several thousand folk from nearby towns paid as extras, heavily costumed, celebrated Marie Antoinette's arrival at Versailles in a carriage costing a hundred and fifty grand, then sang and danced their way through Rain's garden to the throne of France, only to have the director of photography wave his hands. Wrong wrong wrong. The seasonal light was all wrong. They'd simply have to re-shoot. By then, Lena's affair with her married co-star, John Melville, was headline news, and two-thirds of the plants and trees had to be replaced.

HELEN DROVE FROM THE OFFICE to the Chatsworth set more often now, bringing Rain lunch, usually sandwiches and iced tea. His on-set trailer was cramped with seedlings, sketches, and books, with barely room for two to sit without their knees touching. A pokey little fan in the window click-clicked click-clicked click-clicked.

How much longer, did he think?

"Like a horse with a broken leg," Rain said, "but no one wants to put a bullet in its head."

The recent board coup at Vox Pictures had installed a new studio exec who, rumour had it, was going to pull the plug.

"Why not just walk away?"

The shoot kept him away from his empty house. He'd see it through for Lena's sake.

"So you'd rather be here, moping all day in this hot trailer, making yourself sick? Look at you. White as a ghost. You need a boot in the ass."

Sometimes Rain hated her.

Helen took an angry bite of her sandwich. "Have you seen her?"

Meaning Nora.

"No," he said. Nothing after that one piece of gossip Hollywood didn't know about. While Lena and John preoccupied the press with their antics and even the Pope felt the need to weigh in on family values, Nora had helped herself to Lena's jewelry and vanished.

He tossed his sandwich back onto the wax paper, uneaten. "Need to see to the gardens before the day's filming. If they're filming."

"The sooner this elephant dies, the better," said Helen, stretching.

LENA CALLED, LOOKING FOR A friendly face at the New York premiere. I'd love for you to take me, lovie, she told Rain, but the studio, still thinking they could gloss over the affair, insisted Lena and newly divorced John face the crowds together.

Boullian put on a brave face for the press, but told everyone in Lena's hotel room before the premiere that those motherfuckers disembowelled his masterpiece. He meant the new head of Vox who'd recut the film to a marketable length. The director of *Marie!* had not underestimated the carnage. Rain staggered out of the premiere. All his beautiful garden sequences, months of labour, cut, along with most of the other garden shots in the film. Lena's response was more dramatic. When she fled the theatre in a cloud of floral dress, it was to the ladies room where she threw up.

"THANK GOD IT'S YOU," Lena said when she opened the door. "I couldn't stomach the sight of anyone else this morning."

The coffee table in her hotel room was littered with roughly read newspapers. *The Times*, baffled by a tragic story punctuated with campy Busby Berkeley-like dance numbers, at least hinted, perhaps sarcastically, that the film might be ahead of its time. The *Daily News* had turned the studio's marketing slogan, *Lena Sings!* into *Lena Stinks!* Open suitcases littered the room.

"Yes, I'm off to Saint-Tropez. Alone, if you must know. John and I are done. Seems that the chase was the thing for him. Expect you'll be reading about it in the evening papers. Gonna find me a beach where no one knows me."

Rain figured that might be hard. "How long?" he asked.

"Forever, if I have my way. It's not like I can't afford it, huh?"

If *Variety*'s report was true, Lena's overtime had made her several million dollars before her flop even opened.

"So no need for me to call the cops on that little bitch of yours." She tapped Rain on his chest. "Consider those diamonds my parting gift to you."

Falling quiet, she stood, not knowing where to start packing.

*Lilium*

# 1959

The driver slowly backed his truck up the steep incline to Rain's house, delivering the first of two shipments of Italian marble destined for a client's Malibu estate. An older man, recently taken up with a former Disney Mouseketeer half his age. Helen had positively crooned over the lurid details in the scandal magazines. Apparently the groom had a daughter older than the bride. The garden was to be a wedding gift, to keep her happy. Rain had an idea how that would turn out, but he cashed the cheque and got to work.

"Nitwit," said Helen, watching the driver trying to navigate the curve half way up the lane. "Complete idiot."

She'd like nothing better than to yank him out of the truck and back it up herself. But the phone in the house was ringing.

"I'll go," said Rain, waving Helen down the lane after the truck.

"It's probably that Mrs. Lesley next door," Helen grumbled.

Neighbours all around were complaining about trucks coming and going and Rain using his house to store landscaping materials. Helen had been pestering him about an office somewhere. Good deals over on Jefferson Boulevard, she claimed.

"Don't worry. I'll put in that fountain she wants, that'll make her happy," he replied.

"For God's sake, don't you dare tell her you'll do it for free!"

That Helen. Rain smiled as he hurried into the house, amongst boxes piled high and papers scattered about. She could drive a truck better than any man and somehow keep all this mess making money. Sure, maybe she did take up a lot of space, but weeks could pass now without Rain thinking about *them*, how meaningless the days really were, how tired of it all he was. What would he do without her? He picked up the phone. The voice on the line he had dreamt of, longed for, was curt. Nora, calling from San Diego.

"Why haven't you called? It's been ages! Are you all right?" Rain spoke loudly, hurriedly, worriedly, like a father, his hand wrapping itself about the cord. "What are you doing there?"

"If you let me get a word in...it's Mother. You'd better come quick."

HELEN WAS HAVING NONE OF IT. How long had it been since he'd heard from either of them? Three, four years? Now this kid says jump, and Rain asks how high? That girl had no business making a demand like that after how they'd treated him. And the money he'd shelled out for the two of them...just to take off and leave? Not on Helen's watch. Who knows what boobytrap was waiting for him in San Diego! Besides, what about all this marble in the driveway?

"If you've got something on your mind, say it," he said, tossing shirts into a suitcase.

"Why listen to me? You never do."

"So you think I'm a fool?"

"She took up with another man! Let *him* take care of her."

"You don't understand."

"Got that right."

"I have to go."

Then Helen was coming too.

She wanted to stop for dinner, but Rain insisted they drive straight through. When they arrived she answered no, she wasn't coming into the hospital with him. She'd find them rooms in a motel.

In the reflection of the hospital's glass door, her truck peeled away, and Rain was left with a good look at himself—tired and worn. Old. He took a deep breath and stepped inside. Much had changed in the world since he had haunted the halls of Bon Sauveur, and much hadn't. Did all hospitals stink of medicine, urine, the crappy coffee poured robotically from vending machines?

Nora waited in a long row of empty chairs in the hallway. She was unkempt and scratched at her arm, looked like a month of Sunday suppers wouldn't go amiss. Or a bath. Rain didn't know what hurt more, his Nora like this, or not knowing what hell she'd fallen into. She stood, nervously, when she saw him coming.

"What happened?"

"Yeah, nice to see you too, pops."

"I'm sorry—" He wanted to hold her, but that wasn't happening.

"Last guy she lived with dropped her off here. At least he thought enough about her to call me." Nora looked down.

"Is she going to be okay? Are you okay? What have you been doing all this time?"

"Who cares."

"Nora—"

"Look, she's got syphilis, if you must know. I didn't, not until now. She never got it treated. It's in her brain." Tears welled in the corners of Nora's eyes. She was not so tough now.

"Can I see her?"

"She doesn't want to see you."

Rain turned for the ward, but Nora took his hand. "There's something else."

"I don't care."

"I know, but you should."

THE WARD WAS LONG and filled with women in various stages of medicated death. Lily's bed was in the corner, the overhead light switched off. The only sound from behind the curtains was a kind of raspy, halting rattle. The nurse who escorted them looked like a younger version of Sister Wicks: stern and disapproving, with a shorter skirt and thick glasses. She explained that Lily's difficulty breathing was due to the facial tumours. Even with Nora's warning, Rain was not prepared to meet a face uglier than his.

"The doctor's given her something. Don't put too much into what she says," the nurse added as she turned to leave.

Lily was bald, and lay quietly. Rain sat beside the bed, took hold of one of her hands, swollen with grape-sized tumours.

Her eyes flickered.

"I called him, Mama," said Nora.

Rain squeezed her hand, wanted to hold it against his face.

"Don't look at me," she said weakly. The strength in her hand belied her illness. Then she smiled in recognition. "You came. You won't leave?"

"As long as you need me."

She pulled her hand from his, coughed, and looked away.

"You mustn't worry about Nora," he said.

"Why? You think I'm dying?"

"No, I just want you to know I'll take care of her. While you're here."

"Girl can take care of herself. Always has. That's what we do."

"She has me now. I mean, I know she's a grown woman—"

"And who are you?"

"Like you said, remember?"

"Nora, what's he saying? Who is this man?"

Rain took her hand in his. "I'm Nora's father, Lily."

Then she laughed. The kind of laugh that reaches down your throat and squeezes your heart until there's nothing for the blood to do but stop flowing.

"No, no, no." Lily's words were weak and raw but determined. "You? Oh, my darling thing. Saved you for a rainy day." And her misshapen mouth turned up in a revolting grin.

The nurse slipped back through the curtains. The patient had to rest now.

But this was Lily's moment, and by God, she'd say her piece. "You loved me. You wanted to believe, so I let you. Just had to get you drunk."

"Mama—"

"Oh, go...both of you."

But she didn't let go of Rain's hand as her cough worsened, and the nurse reached for her head and offered water.

"No!" She swatted the glass away and turned to Rain. "Wait," and pulling him close, she reached up and touched his tears.

"Enough," ordered the nurse, and ushered them out of the ward.


"I TRIED TO WARN YOU," said Nora, outside.

"Is there nothing to be done?"

"We'll make her comfortable," said the nurse, "but if there are arrangements to make—"

By the row of coffee machines, Nora sank into a chair, then looked angrily at Rain. "You knew. You've always known. It's written all over your face."

"Nora—"

"If there's one thing I know about you, it's that you can't hide anything. You're not surprised by what she said in there. Tell me the truth."

"Yes, I always suspected I wasn't your real father." *But for Christ's sake, look at me, Nora. What woman would love me?*

"How could the both of you make me believe it? All these years?"

"I wanted it to be true—"

"You selfish bastard."

"Nora—"

"She's dying, but you? I thought you were my father."

"I am your father. Blood means nothing to this." Rain pounded his chest. "And the man who was your father, you think he'd be here today?" Save you from the Germans, turn over every stone in Europe looking for you, beg to keep you out of jail, and love you every single day he knew you were alive, no matter what? "It doesn't change how I feel about you."

But Nora buried her face in her hands.

"Nora, please—"

"Just, fucking, go."

The hospital doors swung open. Helen was back for him.


BACK AT HOME HELEN STEPPED out to pick up lunch at the café near Rain's house and returned to find him sitting on a headless Roman centurion in his backyard.

"Why's the phone off the hook?" she asked.

He was surrounded by crates and straw, clay amphorae, chipped busts, heroic torsos, and broken columns. Pieces of empires and destinies and dreams. Lies. It all came from a factory in Italy. Did good work, looked almost as old as the real old stuff,

Helen had said. Except for the sarcophagus. That was definitely Egyptian. The order specified Etruscan, but that was the Italians for you. Can't get a goddamned thing right. All for clients with more money than brains. No one would ever know the truth.

"What am I supposed to do with all this?" he asked her without feeling.

"Huh? What do you mean?"

Rain had planned to sprinkle them about a colonnaded peristyle and atrium, its catch basin tiled in mosaic, and bury pieces here and there, to make the garden look like it'd been a ruin for centuries.

"It's all just pieces of shit."

"And you'll put them together and make something beautiful. That's what you do. Like you always do. Are you all right? Why was the phone off the hook in the kitchen?"

He looked at her blankly. "The hospital called."

NORA MET HIM FOR LUNCH under the Biltmore Hotel's cloistered arches filled with glass, splashing fountains, and mammoth-sized columns. Her hair was unkempt, her clothes matted and hanging off bone. The lids of her eyes were painted green and she pulled out a cigarette as soon as they were seated.

"Thanks for coming. I didn't know if you would," she said.

"I'll always be here for you."

"Yeah. Sure. Sorry about not calling you for the service. Wasn't much, just got her buried. Didn't think you'd want to go all the way down there for it...." She leaned over and took his offer of a light. "I meant to tell you, I saw it you know, your movie."

Rain raised his eyebrows. Ancient history, that.

"Art house around the corner was showing it. Line outside every night. Better than I thought it would be. What are you doing now?"

"Long done with Hollywood, but I'll be okay."

"Good. I mean, I'm glad for you. You with Helen now?"

"What do you mean?"

Nora, anxious, tumbled her cigarette ash on the white linen tablecloth. She really didn't give a shit who Rain was with. She wanted a thousand dollars.

"What happened to Lena's necklace?"

"Oh fuck. Be like that then—"

"Sit down, Nora."

She looked around. Fumbled the lighting of another cigarette. "Cops ever find out?"

"No, thanks to Lena. Are you high?"

"Just something to take the edge off. Christ. I've lost my mother, you know. Well? Will you give it to me? You owe me that much."

Rain was thankful to have to bring out his wallet, find one of the cheques he carried. She'd not see his disappointment.

"Thanks. So, I guess this is goodbye."

"It doesn't have to be. Nothing's changed," he said. "About how I feel."

But Nora had to run. She shoved an envelope towards him on the table, some papers relating to Lily, she said. By the arches, fountains, and mammoth-sized columns, she turned and looked back. "You look tired, pops. Take care of yourself."

*Eucalyptus globulus*

# 1961

Rain looked up from inside his truck at the three-storey peeling and pitted sand-coloured sphinx, surrounded by asphalt cracked with weeds. The door to the abandoned movie house, between the giant paws, was boarded over. The ticket booth long gone.

"So? What do you think?" asked Helen as she stepped out the other side of his truck.

Rain didn't know what he was supposed to think. "I used to watch movies here. Didn't know it was still around."

"It was a car dealership for a bit, and a bingo hall. I want to turn it into a garden centre." She watched him closely. "We'll sell push mowers, bedding plants, furniture, even sculpture, but not that shit *you* buy. Everything people need for a garden."

"Why would I do that?"

"So you don't have to work so much, or as hard. We can make more money here running this place. Nine to five. No driving all over southern California."

"But what about my clients?"

"No one's saying you can't take some on. Just maybe not so many."

Most of the building's stucco face was gone. A man on a ladder was gingerly tapping at what remained.

"Helen—"

"Hear me out. All those new suburbs they're building in the valley, those people want lawns and gardens and they'll drive by this place every day getting into Los Angeles. We can sell them everything they need. Big sign, right there. I've even got a name. Starlight Gardens. Don't you see how great an opportunity this is?"

"What about my crew?"

"Those Mexicans shouldn't even be in this country, but give some of 'em work here if you must."

"What about the office?" They leased a Culver City space, on Jefferson Boulevard. The Pasadena house had to be sold to pay for Lily's hospital bills and burial. "We've barely been there a year."

"What good's a lease if you don't break it?"

Rain was shaking his head. "I'm a gardener, not a shopkeeper."

"Yes, but you haven't enjoyed it much lately. Not since—" Nora. Two years now. Ungrateful, thieving slut—and that was Helen being kind. Probably lying dead somewhere with a needle in her arm. "And then there's your heart."

"Ah, leave it. I'm fine."

"I know, I know, but just think what a great opportunity this could be. You could take vacations. I saw you reading that *National Geographic*, about France. Maybe you could even get yourself a dog. Good exercise walking a dog—"

Rain pulled his hat off, wiped his head with a soiled handkerchief. By now Helen knew this was his give-me-time-to-think gesture, the one that really meant he wasn't going to think about it at all.

"I wouldn't be good for a dog," he said.

The man on the ladder let them know that he had done those

elephants in *Intolerance.* "Big picture in its day, if you like silent movies. You folks see it? I could do a face. Someone you'd like? Put my wife's on one of those elephants for Griffith. How 'bout yours, mister?"

Rain didn't think so.

Helen wanted to know if buddy was going to chat all day or get on with the estimate for the building's repairs.

"You leave it with me, little lady. I think I know just the right face."

"Helen, nobody's going to come to a—garden store."

"Why not? Why live in California if you're not going to be outside? People moving into cookie-cutter houses can't afford what you charge. But they can afford a picnic table, some flowers. We could even sell Christmas trees. Every season, they'll be back and we can teach them how to plant new things."

"Teach myself out of a job, you mean."

"Fix the place up, get the right products in, we can make more money here in a week than we do now in a month. Two months. There's even space inside for an office. And deep down, you know I'm right."

"About what?"

"Time to move on."

HELEN SAID THAT THIS TIME she meant it: she wasn't coming back.

The phone rang, no one answered. The mail was already piling up, unopened. Rain sat uncomfortably in the chair reserved for visitors, glanced at his watch. Morning came brightly through the partially closed Venetian blinds, filling the office with washed-out yellow light thick with dust. Plans and faded pencil sketches and maps taped to the walls, lists of phone numbers, folders leaking paper, Helen's half-empty cup of coffee, the desiccated cornflower in a glass jar. He'd tossed it on her desk weeks before, coming back from a garden in Carmel, and she'd smiled, said they were her favourite because they lasted forever. She had a beautiful smile, a grateful smile, the kind that expected nothing in return.

Only yesterday she'd been sitting here, going through the morning mail. "Ann Margaret heard you were the best in town and she's just bought a new house. Well la-de-da for the rest of us mortals. And the city wants you to consult on the parks."

Rain asked if there was any milk for the coffee.

"You look tired. Still not sleeping? I'll run across the street and get some."

He told her not to bother. Another day hot and dry enough to make you believe winter wasn't around the corner. Her going outside could wait.

"Did you see the For Sale sign on the way in? MGM's selling off the back lots," she said.

"No one makes movies here anymore." Rain opened the blinds and watched as cars stopped at the light outside.

"You're in a funny mood," Helen said. "Maybe this'll cheer you. That reporter called again."

"What did you tell him?"

"Same as always, but you could talk to the guy." She sipped her coffee.

"I'm as sick of that bloody movie now as I was years ago."

"He says the studio that bought the rights wants to reissue a director's cut for television. Including the lost minutes of your garden."

"So?"

"People will finally see it."

"On tiny black and white screens in their living room while they eat TV dinners."

Rain went over to the open doorway to smoke.

"Doctor said you should quit."

His still-lit cigarette bounced off the pavement.

When the phone rang, Helen had been reminding him not to forget the appointment tomorrow with that client in West Hollywood. Cordell Drive. Hilltop surrounding an apartment building wanted landscaping. The address sounded familiar.

"Helen?"

She was still on the phone but slowly standing, as if at attention.

"What's wrong?"

She pulled the receiver away, then covered it with her hand. "It's Mrs. Kennedy's secretary."

"I don't know any Kennedy."

"Mrs. *First Lady* Kennedy."

He frowned, confused. "What do they want?"

"She says the President's wife loved what you did at Marjorie Winston's. She wants to talk to you about doing her garden."

"Where?"

"At the White House."

When Helen hung up the phone they stared at one another in amazed silence.

*Washington.*

But of course, he couldn't consider it, Helen said, just like that. Keeping up the Rose Garden meant years...every blade of grass under scrutiny, just so the next First Lady could rip it out and start over. And apartments were fabulously expensive in DC, she was sure of it. He'd suffered two heart attacks already.

"Jesus, Helen, what's the harm in at least thinking about going east?"

"What about our store?"

"I told you. I'm not a shopkeeper."

"Then I'm done," she had said. "I'm not picking up your pieces anymore."

But Helen always came back. With pie as an apology. That's what Helen did.

Only this time, she didn't.

THE MORNING HUMMED AND RATTLED with air conditioners. Outside, a hazy, unseasonable autumn sat low and dirty and dry. Weeks of it now. Rain glanced at his watch. He was still early, but feeling late. Sweat darkened his shirt. He pulled his truck off Santa Monica Boulevard, swung up Cordell Drive, parked in front of the apartments under a tree, its trunk grey and yellow with lichen. If Rain hadn't been thinking about Helen, he might have remembered where he was.

He riffled around in the glovebox, in the console. He knew it was here, it had to be, buried under matchbooks, lunch wrappers, an old Singapore Sling recipe scrawled on a cocktail napkin, broken sunglasses, Helen's missing glove, restaurant mints, seed catalogues, stubs from a rainy day matinee of *Exodus*.

Lose your head if it wasn't screwed on, Helen would say if she were here, easily finding the client's worksheet where he'd left it, tucked among lipstick-stained bits of her.

But she wasn't here. Only his face in the rear-view mirror looking back, looking worn, and tired of atoning.

The client was late, there was no sign of anyone. Rain got out of his truck, untangled the fraying old scarf about his neck, wiped his brow, and tossed it in the back. He glanced at his watch again. Up here the breeze was light and cool, and Helen was right. Right about everything. He wasn't blind. He knew she loved him, had always loved him, but she wasn't Lily. A few blocks back there was a pay phone. He could get in the truck, turn around, and call, call until she answered. Tell her he knew what he wanted now because he could see the city rolling like a quilt to the sea and it was enough. He could make something beautiful and lasting right here.

And because she was not Lily, Rain did not love her, but when the cicada warned loud and long overhead, and the sun was cut quickly through by the blue-green leaves of the eucalyptus, he knew, if given one more chance, he would.

HELEN BROUGHT HER SWEATER and hung it on the coat rack behind her chair. She placed the newspapers on top of the lease to the old movie theatre. She lit her first Tareyton, made coffee. She was late because of the Washington papers. She'd gone looking elsewhere when the newsagent on Jefferson didn't carry them.

The smell of coffee revived her, and she opened the blinds. Ran her fingers over the papery petals of the cornflower on her desk and glanced at her watch.

At 10:37 A.M. the phone rang.

"Miss Hepner?"

The man identified himself as a police officer. He sounded young. He'd answered a call that morning up on Cordell Drive, the old Cukor property.

"I'm sorry, ma'am, there's been an accident. Falling branch—"

And the rest did not matter.

## ALSO BY
## STEPHENS GERARD MALONE

*Big Town*

*I Still Have a Suitcase in Berlin*

*Miss Elva*